PRAISE FOR

I'M A FOOL TO WANT YOU

"A breathtaking, remarkable collection of stories. The boundaries between what is real and what is fantastical collapse, providing a haunting series of characters whose presence lingers long after we've closed the book, forcing us to consider sex, desire, humor, justice, and dignity in a completely new way."
— Cleyvis Natera, author of *Neruda on the Park*

"Camila Sosa Villada is such a beautiful writer! This book blazes, charms, disquiets, and breaks your heart—you'll regret it if you don't read it."
— Casey Plett, author of *Little Fish* and *A Dream of a Woman*

"Stunning. A collection as bright and sparkling as the precious stones one character believes she can find at the heart of a pomegranate. Camila Sosa Villada spins tales of mythic revenge, of magics great and small, and of finally finding sanctuary—in a sibling's bed, a homemade scone, a sudden jungle. Tenderly crafted and captivating, these stories offer a sanctuary in themselves."
— Morgan Thomas, author of *Manywhere: Stories*

"Original and imaginatively wide-ranging."
— *Electric Literature*

"After I finished reading Camila's story, it kept growing in me...As a story of gender oppression, *Bad Girls* (beautifully translated by Kit Maude) would sound familiar almost everywhere...To record the *travesti* experience, no matter how harrowingly painful, as something precious is [its] purpose." —*The New Yorker*

"Every so often, a slim book absolutely clobbers you with its exuberance and beauty—for me, this was that book."   —Torrey Peters, author of *Detransition, Baby*

"This is an important book: fun, tragic, political, and full of marvel. It makes you understand the lives of these women and the wonder and pain of being different and rejected. It's full of pride and exquisitely written. It will break your heart and at the same time make you want to laugh and dance, full of love and sorrow."
    —Mariana Enríquez, author of *Our Share of Night*

"A beautiful novel, moving, disturbing, raw, and honest. In skillfully rendered language, charged with poetic energy, it takes us deep into the world of trans prostitution and explores the violent and tender bonds that unite the women who inhabit it."
    —Fernanda Melchor, author of *Hurricane Season*

"Remarkable...*Bad Girls* is a generational testimony as well as a personal one. It imagines a future and exorcises a past, being exceptional for what it promises and for the portrait of a life it leaves behind."
    —*Astra Magazine*

I'M A FOOL TO WANT YOU

I'M A FOOL
TO WANT YOU

Stories

CAMILA SOSA VILLADA

Translated from the Spanish by Kit Maude

OTHER PRESS
NEW YORK

Originally published in Spanish as *Soy una tonta por quererte*
in 2022 by Tusquets Editores S.A., Buenos Aires
Copyright © 2022, Camila Sosa Villada
Copyright © 2022, Tusquets Editores S.A.
2022 Latin American Rights Agency – Grupo Planeta
English translation copyright © 2024, Kit Maude

Production editor: Yvonne E. Cárdenas
Text designer: Jennifer Daddio / Bookmark Design & Media Inc.
This book was set in Baskerville MT Pro and Intro Head R UC G Base
by Alpha Design & Composition of Pittsfield, NH

1 3 5 7 9 10 8 6 4 2

Library of Congress Cataloging-in-Publication Data
Names: Sosa Villada, Camila, author. | Maude, Kit, translator.
Title: I'm a fool to want you : stories / Camila Sosa Villada ; translated from
the Spanish by Kit Maude.
Other titles: Soy una tonta por quererte. English | I am a fool to want you
Description: New York : Other Press, 2024.
Identifiers: LCCN 2023043463 (print) | LCCN 2023043464 (ebook) |
ISBN 9781635423853 (paperback) | ISBN 9781635423860 (ebook)
Subjects: LCSH: Sosa Villada, Camila—Translations into English. |
LCGFT: Short stories.
Classification: LCC PQ7798.429.O757 S6913 2024 (print) |
LCC PQ7798.429.O757 (ebook) | DDC 863/.7—dc23/eng/20231002
LC record available at https://lccn.loc.gov/2023043463
LC ebook record available at https://lccn.loc.gov/2023043464

CONTENTS

THANK YOU,
DIFUNTA CORREA

Late in November 2008, Don Sosa and La Grace visited the shrine to the Difunta Correa in Vallecito, just under sixty miles from the town of San Juan. It wasn't yet dawn when La Grace put the thermos of hot water into the basket along with the rest of the maté drinking paraphernalia, the scones she'd baked the day before to eat on the journey, the *milanesa* sandwiches, a cool box with soda and a few cans of beer for Don Sosa, and, in her handbag, a silver medallion I was given at school as a reward for being a good student.

Don Sosa got jumpy when he knew he had to drive any significant distance. All week he'd been checking the car, making sure that the engine was running perfectly, taking it apart, making replacements, swapping out old tubes for new ones, trying to guarantee that he wasn't going to have any trouble on the road so he wouldn't have to pay the bribes that the highway police of Cuyo customarily demand of tourists. La Grace would make scenes that ended in fiery arguments over the mess Don Sosa made of his clothes during his fussing. His pants got covered in grease; big black blotches would appear on his shirt. It didn't matter what he was wearing: if his car needed to pop its hood for a checkup, he'd roll up his sleeves and pretend he was a mechanic. "And I'm the idiot left doing the laundry," La Grace grumbled.

They set out from Mina Clavero and crossed the Traslasierra Valley listening to folk music, drinking maté, joking with one another like a couple used to traveling, a couple who enjoys traveling. They'd gotten used to long journeys when I went off to study in Córdoba and they got back together after being separated for a year. However, the destination was new; they'd never been to the shrine to the Difunta Correa before.

The heat in Villa Dolores made them grumpy and as the sun started to climb in the sky around La Rioja, they began to squabble over nothing, nonsense arguments that never ended.

Don Sosa was a good driver. And he made masterful use of bad language on the road. Whenever another driver did something wrong, he'd curse their entire families, including their mothers, grandmothers, and sisters. Sometimes he went as far as wishing death upon them and La Grace scolded him like a child.

"You can't go around swearing like that. Don't you ever get bored of it?"

Whenever they passed a cross by the side of the road commemorating a fatal accident, or a statue to a saint, then Don Sosa would cross himself and pray:

"Curita Brochero, accompany us on our journey. Amen. Gauchito Gil, protect us on our journey. Virgincita of the Valley, I entrust myself to you."

La Grace couldn't stand her husband's corny piety. She had been hurt by the Catholic Church. She once went to mass, on my first day as an altar boy when it was my job to hold the wafers for Father Pedernera as he administered Communion to the congregation. She'd been to confession and was made a little nervous by the sight of her boy helping the priest behind the altar. When it was her turn, instead of receiving the flesh and blood of Christ, a wafer and a sip of wine, from a couple of steps above, she was met with a hairy hand nudging her to one side. And she heard the priest's voice:

"You can't receive Communion."

"Why?" La Grace asked, her enormous eyes beginning to brim over.

"Because you're living in sin."

La Grace withdrew without saying a word and chain-smoked cigarettes on the steps of the Church of Perpetual Mercy of Mina Clavero until the mass was over and I came out. As we walked our bicycles down the hill, La Grace, with the same painful glimmer in her eyes she'd had when challenging the priest, said:

"I'm never going back."

She never went back to mass and, little by little, grew angrier with Catholicism. She kept the faith in the Virgin of the Valley she'd inherited from her grandmother, but turned her back on the beliefs that had guided her life so far.

I'm not sure how, but many years later, they heard about the Difunta Correa. Maybe it traveled on the winds, the Zonda in the west passing it on to its peers farther east, but news of Deolinda's great power reached my parents. They must have regarded it as something pagan, something that had somehow broken free of the bonds of Catholicism. And one day they went to see her.

Deolinda Correa is a popular saint who one night, before she started to work miracles, harassed and abused by the violent town drunk, was forced to flee with her newborn baby in her arms. She tried to cross the desert from Angaco, heading for La Rioja, where her husband had been taken by the Montonera guerrillas during the civil war in the 1840s. She wouldn't have had more than a few drops of water on her. Just her fear and the baby. Her desperation overwhelmed her rational side and she suddenly found herself running in *alpargata* espadrilles through the desert on a night so bright you could see underground. The desert is treacherous. Once you've run out of water and you're walking under the hateful sun and you get lost and someone at your breast is crying and you begin to regret having fled from the bastard who pestered you into slipping away like a rat in the night, all you can do is give up. Curse your idiot of a husband, say that's enough, and surrender to the elements. Let the exhaustion and thirst have their way with you. Clasping your son against your breast. Taking your last delirious breaths in the glare of sunbeams bouncing spitefully back off the hot sand.

Dark, ominous scavengers circled over Deolinda's lifeless body. Shepherds saw the ring of death from afar, thinking that a goat or sheep had succumbed in the desert, and headed toward the gathered buzzards.

But it wasn't an animal they found. They found a dead Deolinda Correa with her baby still at her breast, suckling, oblivious to the tragic scene all around him. That was the first miracle. After that, the Difunta Correa came to symbolize a sainthood that eluded the Catholic Church, and the foundations were laid for a very humble shrine at which the poor professed their faith with offerings. Toy houses, wedding dresses, plastic flowers, silver and bronze plaques, watches, earrings, crosses, photographs, and bottles of water.

So what were Don Sosa and La Grace on their way there for in late 2008, crossing an entire desert in a run-down Renault 18? They were going to ask the saint to find their travesti daughter a better job. What was their travesti daughter's profession? She was a prostitute, of course. She'd gone to Córdoba to study communications and theater but had ended up a whore. They didn't know this, but in the winter of that year, a pair of johns had strangled their daughter until she'd passed out and stolen all of her meager possessions: an old television that had lost its color, a borrowed DVD, a hi-fi, and her cell phone charger. Also, the forty pesos she had in her handbag. The thieves had tied her up with her own clothes while she was still passed out and then used a kitchen knife to threaten her as they both fucked her, not too rough, but all through the night. The next day, a taxi driver friend came by to pick them up and they left her tied up and humiliated in her room in the boardinghouse.

Don Sosa and La Grace had no idea about the cocktails of drugs their daughter needed to get to sleep, or to numb her senses, or how barren her days were, her days in the wilderness. People say that mothers know everything. But this was beyond La Grace's experience. In her housewife's heart, there was room only for the suspicion that her daughter wasn't well, that maybe she was mixed up in murky business, but the word "prostitution" was anathema and she refused to think any further about it. Don Sosa's denial wasn't so complete. Which was why he was so angry with his daughter.

La Grace says that the day they visited the shrine to the Difunta Correa, she wept when she saw the first pilgrim climbing the hill on his knees, tears running from his eyes. She imagined the promises that that had been made, the prayers for a house, for an operation to go well, for a dream job, for a great love to return, and it moved her. She and Don Sosa had cried together, because in their impotence they now found themselves in the middle of the desert, asking a saint to do something they'd been unable to do for themselves. After lunch, Don Sosa and La Grace climbed the hill to the altar where an image of the Difunta Correa stands surrounded by the wedding dresses that supplicants have left in payment for the delivered miracle. They were carrying plastic bottles of water and that small medal, which their travesti daughter had won in high school.

"Help her to get a good job, Difuntita Correa. Help her to get away from what she's doing now and change her life."

Outside, the Zonda swirled around and then gusted forth to soar across the deserts that had scorched the fleeing Deolinda. All the way to the city of Córdoba.

Three months later, the travesti daughter of Don Sosa and La Grace, me in other words—in literature you can't disguise a first person, the phrases start to wither three or four paragraphs in—made her debut in *Carnival Flesh*. Because in addition to being a hooker, I also loved the theater. Maria, one of my best friends, invited me to take part in her drama thesis. It consisted of mounting a production and then giving it a theoretical framework. We asked Paco Giménez, our third-year acting teacher at the drama school, to be our advisor and set about brewing the potion that would become *Carnival Flesh*. We gave it an ironic subtitle: *A Stage Portrait of a Travesti*. But people didn't understand the irony. The play told the story of how my parents, and my hometown, had taken my decision to become a travesti. On Paco

Giménez's suggestion, we combined the biographical narrative with a few characters from the plays of Federico García Lorca. It took us almost a year and a half to get our monstrous creation on its feet. Sometimes Maria would come by the boardinghouse to take me to rehearsal after a bad night and find me looking worse than Christ on the cross, my eyes gunked with mascara, traces of other people's drool all over my body, absolutely ravenous. We'd have something to eat in the theater and then get to work interspersing scenes from my adolescence with texts by García Lorca.

"A travesti knows what it is to be lonely, like Doña Rosita the Spinster. A travesti knows about dictatorship and repression, like in *The House of Bernarda Alba*. Don't some travestis yearn to be mothers like Yerma? And don't they have tragic love affairs, like in *Blood Wedding*? Travestis have been shot and murdered like Federico García Lorca himself," Paco said, and we racked our brains, determined to get it right, to make a good play.

Once, during a rehearsal, he said to me, "I know the color of your soul. It's translucent."

Carnival Flesh lasted about fifty minutes and ended with me in the nude, standing in front of an audience who couldn't believe they were seeing a travesti do such a thing. Maria got her degree in theater with top grades and plenty of praise. The play hadn't cost us very much to put on. I'd made the costumes myself, we didn't use many props: a few false mustaches, some plastic flowers, and a bridal tiara. We'd planned to hold eight performances over two months. One a week.

Friends, relatives, and fellow students came to the first one. About thirty people. Fifty came to the next. The audience for the third was eighty, and by the fourth we were having to turn people away at the door.

Carnival Flesh made its debut in March 2009. Three months after my parents' pledge to the Difunta Correa. The reviews were excellent. I was interviewed on television and in the newspapers. Word of mouth spread about the play and people who'd never set foot in a theater in their life came to see what all the fuss was about. Crowds formed at the entrance to every theater we performed at. I began to think that I could make it as an actress. I was tired of hustling and life had demonstrated to me on several occasions that I wasn't smart enough to make it as a prostitute. Maybe now was the time to try my luck. I used my earnings from the theater to pay the months of rent I owed at the boardinghouse and replaced everything those bastards had stolen from me the year before. I never imagined that La Grace and

Don Sosa had made a promise to the Difunta Correa on my behalf. Apparently, it had worked, because just like Mamma Roma, I said *"Addio, bambole,"* and left prostitution with a swing of my hips to live off the box office instead of my johns' wallets.

Was this what I needed? And was it one of the Difunta's miracles? Was being an actress better than being a prostitute? I don't know. I'm pretty sure that I didn't have the knack for making money with my ass. I was gullible and lazy, I didn't know how to sharpen my instincts, I didn't have tits. I was, all in all, a terrible whore. And I was sad, and suffered because I was young and easy prey for tragedy. Maybe now things would be different. Maybe now I'd do things better. But during those years, when the miracle happened, I met with only disappointment. Sometimes, when I'm in the mood to be cruel to myself, Don Sosa, and La Grace, I wonder whether a simple telephone call wouldn't have sufficed. But they went to the Difunta Correa and the disaster that was my life got put back together in dressing rooms and stages, traveling across the country like a twentieth-century theatrical troupe, taking the allure of the Mediterranean to unsuspecting venues such as Itá Ibaté and Bouwer.

A short time later, La Grace, Don Sosa, and I went to thank the Difunta for helping me to turn a corner. Before we got into my father's Renault 18, we promised each other that we'd be nice on the trip. As a family, we weren't very good at being trapped together in a confined space. And we kept our word.

"Look at this desert, honey. It's no wonder the poor Difunta died of thirst," said La Grace, passing me the maté gourd.

"And it gets so cold at night," added Don Sosa.

At the shrine, I was moved by the sight of the pilgrims, just as my mother had been on her first visit. The way they used their bodies to atone for affairs of the spirit. When you get down to it, you can be as mystical and saintly as you like, but it always comes back to working the flesh. I also noticed how extraordinarily sexy the plaster image of the Difunta Correa was. When I saw it, it occurred to me that the bombshell Coca Sarli would have been the perfect person to play her in the movie.

"The Difunta is hot!" I whispered to La Grace. We got the giggles and Don Sosa led us out. Out in the light, we could see that he'd been crying.

La Grace saw *Carnival Flesh* many times. Don Sosa just the once, four years after its debut. He saw it in Catamarca. The tour just happened to coincide with their now annual trip to see the Difunta Correa. When the show was over, La Grace came to the dressing room looking very worried.

"Your father's nose bled all the way through the show. He went to the bathroom to take off his shirt, it's covered in blood. I think he got anxious." Her voice broke. "It's a difficult play for us," she explained to the troupe.

Her tone was apologetic.

I, meanwhile, had lost my voice. It had never happened to me before. I don't know if the tour had tired me out or I was nervous about acting in front of my father, but right at the start I had to ask for a microphone because no one could hear me. That night the gremlins danced viciously around me, snapping at my heels. After a while, as I was finishing getting dressed and packing up my things, the bad old man I had for a father shyly reappeared. He was burdened with shame. He'd bled through the play, in silence, taking his Lorcan lumps. No one had ever spoken to him like that without getting a beating in return. But his travesti, prostitute daughter, the reason he'd made his promise to the Difunta, was telling him her version of the miracle.

And what happened to the Difunta Correa's son? He was found by the travestis of Sarmiento Park.

DON'T SPEND TOO LONG
IN THE DUST

Martín's legs dangle over the ditch. He's sitting with his new dog, a mongrel puppy with milk-tea fur, just hanging out, which is exactly the activity that pisses his dad off the most. But he loves the afternoon; he wishes it lasted longer so he could stay there doing nothing on the edge of town. The ditch is close to home. He won't have far to go to get back to the chores his father leaves on a list he sticks to the refrigerator with a magnet before leaving for work at the building site. Martin knows exactly how long he can wait before someone starts asking, Where's that little shit got to now?

Today the solitude he so enjoys has been brought to an end. He's holding a new pet, a friend. It's only right to be polite and show him the things he finds beautiful. The ditch close to home, the remains of an abandoned quarry, the hot afternoon, and the concert given by the crickets. Martin is a part of this landscape. He knows it like his own flesh and isn't fooled by nature's appearances: he knows that a rattlesnake or angry scorpion might be lurking behind every flowering bush. He strides through this territory like its lord and master but stays wary, just as his father taught him.

He didn't have to think too hard about his dog's name. He called him Don José after the janitor at school, whom he likes very much because he's always nice to Martín and defends him when one of the big kids decides to pick on him during recess. He knew what he'd call his dog the day that his father gave them the news:

"Mommy has gone, she's taken her things and left us."

He and his sister—who looks so much like her mother—didn't know what to say.

"So don't get sad, pick out something you like, not too expensive, and I'll bring it home when I go into town."

The siblings didn't say a word.

"What do you want?"

Martincito, sharp as a tack, pictured himself with long hair in one of his mother's dresses, trotting through the fields of dust with a dog trailing behind, its tongue lolling out of its mouth.

"I want a doggie. A doggie I can call Don José."

"We'll see," his father said evasively.

And now, before bringing it home, he realizes that he finally has a dog like the one on the calendar in the town's ice cream parlor. A puppy that looks as though it's smiling while a happy blond girl hugs it in a park so green it hurts your eyes. Martincito has always liked going to the ice cream parlor not so much for the ice cream as to gaze at the very image of his desire, the way we all have at one time or another. And here he is now, sitting on the edge of a ditch, having realized that desire, a sensation that feels a little like melancholy. Don José is asleep on his lap, still a puppy, his sweat wetting the boy's legs. He muses that a life as small as his dog's, if thrown down below, would smash to pieces at the bottom the way his sister once crushed a toad with her father's mallet. His sister isn't mean, she just wanted to see what it looked like inside. Their father said that run-over toads were like pomegranates squashed in the asphalt and although she'd never seen a pomegranate, their father had told them that it was the only fruit in the world full of precious stones. It must have made her curious, because his sister would never ordinarily hurt an animal; quite the contrary. At home she doted on the chickens, the goats, and their father's horse.

The afternoon is like an eclipse. If you stare into the horizon, a white spot forms in your eyes that remains in everything you look at afterward. Wherever you look. On one side you can smell the night approaching; on the other the light is intense and orangey.

Children deserve solitude like this sometimes, a maternal silence, a paternal silence that allows them to settle their thoughts staring into the afternoon with their dog, who occasionally lets out a sigh to mark the passage of time. Martincito jumps at the cry of a bird; he's been daydreaming. Don José is young, just two months old, and Martincito met him a few days after he was born, at the home of Doña Rita, his neighbor.

"Aren't they cute?"

"Yes. Where's their mother?"

"She's over there, poor thing, exhausted. She was giving birth all afternoon. I didn't know how to help her. She's resting now." Then she added: "Do you like any of them?"

Martín looked back into the box lined with a checkered blanket his neighbor, who lived about a mile away, was holding out to him and saw it. A puppy whose complicated ancestry had bequeathed long ears that flopped over his eyes like flaps and a wide snout with a rubbery nose.

"That one," said Martín. Inside the box, the dogs whined. Doña Rita was looking at them as reverently as the boy. She took the puppy out of the box and placed it in his hands.

"It's yours if you want it."

"My dad won't," the boy answered.

"You leave the silly man to me."

The mother groaned and barked at Martín to put the puppy back in the box. She was a fat, old bitch who inspired no pity so you didn't feel bad about taking one of her children away. The neighbor, Doña Rita, felt great pity for the boy and was a little sorry that his mother had left like that, in the middle of the night, but she also knew that Ricardo Camacho, the father, was a sour, abusive husband and that something definitive was bound to happen sooner or later. Widowed and almost seventy, Doña Rita had been the only witness to the deterioration of Martín's parents' marriage, from a prudent distance. She would intervene or stay quiet as the circumstances, which were often extreme, warranted. Pain, beatings, chases through the bush, machete in hand. Doña Rita's involvement, having been Martín's mother's confidante, meant that she continued to keep an eye on Ricardo Camacho's home. She lived on her husband's pension. He had been a magistrate in the San Javier district and a father figure to Martincito's mother. When the boy got back from school, he did her shopping for her and carried the bags with a strength and sense of responsibility unheard of in a boy his age. He spoke like an adult and asked questions that made her think.

"Today, at school, some kids laughed when the teacher said 'homosexual' and got sent out of class...What is a homosexual?" he'd asked one day, enjoying the tea at which he was the guest of honor.

Doña Rita was left open-mouthed.

"It's when a girl, instead of liking a boy, likes another girl. And vice versa, when a boy, instead of liking a girl, likes a boy."

"And is that good or bad?"

"It's bad for an old lady like me to be answering these questions."

"But is it good or bad?"

"Personally, I don't think there's anything wrong with it. It depends on the person, some people think it's good, some bad...it scares some people, and some people just don't care. Now, finish your cocoa before it gets cold."

And because she was a woman of her word, soon afterward she went to Martincito's house to talk to his father and tell him that she had a spare puppy and if he wanted, and if she had his father's permission, she would give it to the boy as a birthday present.

"It's the perfect time, his mother has just taught him his first lesson, he's weaned. He'll be a fast learner."

"Big dog?" asked Ricardo Camacho, his chest puffed under a tight, sweat-drenched T-shirt. Underneath was a mass of hard, hairy flesh, a rustic body that drew sighs from the girls in town but that Doña Rita found rather pitiable. Showing off for her! She could be his grandmother and didn't she know it! Looking the other way, she answered:

"The mother's big but who knows what dog saw to her. I don't think he'll get any bigger than this," she said, lowering her palm to knee height. Hunched over like that, she looked older than she was.

"I don't know, small dogs make a lot of trouble. It'll distract the boy."

"But Martincito is such a good student. He can read like an adult, at seven years old! He could use a friend."

"Don't call him Martincito."

"Why not?

"Because it's childish. He needs to grow into a man. You talk to him like a child and the faggot doesn't speak like a man."

"Oh, I am sorry. He's young, he's been through a tough time. He could do with someone who loves him, to keep him company."

Ricardo Camacho stuck his shovel into the earth as though he were drawing a line. The marks he made in the earth spoke to the distance he'd always wanted to put between himself and the old busybody but had never been able to.

"Did the boy ask you to talk to me?"

"No. I thought of it myself. He's very dear to me, he's a good kid."

"Are you sure?" asked Ricardo, narrowing his eyes and turning away slightly to emphasize his mistrust.

"I'm an old woman, Camacho...I wouldn't lie to you."

In the house having his tea, Martincito watched the scene through the curtain in the door, long strips of transparent plastic of the kind found in butcher shops. His eleven-year-old sister, Irupé, was busy darning the elastic in a pair of panties.

"Did you tell her to talk to Dad?" she whispered.

The boy shook his head. When he looked back outside, he saw that he'd missed the end of the conversation and the neighbor was walking back home. His father came back inside, leaving the shovel leaning on the doorframe.

"Did you ask her for the dog?"

The boy shook his head, looking at the ground. Irupé looked at her father; the father looked back at Irupé. This adolescent with the long dark hair was the spitting image of his wife. She was so similar that it scared him sometimes.

"You didn't give him anything for his birthday. Let him have the dog."

Ricardo Camacho looked at his children, who were staring at him fearfully. Abandoned by their mother like they were nothing. He sighed and rubbed his head with both hands, trying to decide what to do; whether to punish his son for asking the old woman for the dog, punish his daughter for talking to him like a grown-up (which she'd been doing a lot lately), or just let the kid have his pup.

"Fine, go fetch it. And when you get back I want you to sieve this whole wheelbarrow of sand, okay?"

He pointed to a mountain of sand, which stood taller than Martincito himself. It would take him all afternoon and into the night to sieve the whole batch. "Then put it in bags, I have to take them to the clinic tomorrow." Ricardo was building an extension to the town clinic.

"Yes, Dad."

He gulped down the last of his maté tea and stood up to hug his father, brimming over with gratitude. Ricardo eased him away brusquely and mechanically, like a crane.

"I don't want it inside the house, understand?"

Martincito nodded.

"And you're in charge of feeding it and if it bothers me even once with its barking, it goes back to the old woman, all right?"

Martincito ran off to get his rickety bike to fetch Don José. In his hurry, he forgot to swerve around the patch of quicksand in front of the house and the back wheel got stuck. He fell into the accursed dust. His father watched from the house.

"The little idiot. Make me some maté, why don't you," he ordered Irupé, and sat down at the table, bathed in sweat, irritated by the dirty mug his son hadn't washed, angry at himself for giving in to the old woman. Irupé put the kettle on and made him the maté. She moved the same way as her mother. Ricardo didn't at all like the relationship between Doña Rita and his son. She'd already been a bad influence on his wife, and events were repeating themselves. She loaned him books. What kind of a friendship was that? The boy needed friends his own age, running off to hunt birds with slingshots or fish in the river, not a froufrou old woman who served him tea and gave him dogs. There were too many women in the boy's life, one who never went away because she'd left already and the other because she'd given him a dog. A shovel and a pickaxe would have been better. But what could he do? Ever since his wife had left it was all he could manage to put food on the table and send the kids to school. He felt sorry for them. He wasn't unaware that, at times, he was a bastard to his children.

It was very true that the girl was like her mom, Antonia Charras. The same hair color, the same mouth and teeth, the same eyes. A maternal inheritance. Antonia Charras worked as the secretary to the town magistrate for fifteen years. Doña Rita, the neighbor, was the magistrate's wife and loved her like her own, as though she'd given birth to her. When she was twenty-two, Antonia met Ricardo Camacho. At the time, he was one of the most handsome men in the area. He had a black Gilera motorbike that roared down the terrible roads, even making it across the quicksand, good soccer legs, and thick arms nourished by meat slaughtered in the garden. His whole body crowed with strength. She, on the other hand, was one of those girls who didn't get much attention from boys.

Maybe it was her pale skin and modest style of dress, which hid her figure; maybe it was the fact that she was the magistrate's secretary, which made her seem untouchable. Maybe it was her flat chest, who knows. But one morning Ricardo Camacho noticed her when he came to the courthouse to do some paperwork for his motorbike, and he liked what he saw of Antonia Charras. For all the aforementioned qualities: her modesty, the shapeless dresses, the flat chest, her ghostly air. He was young but it would be more pertinent to note that he had old-fashioned attitudes. He knew he was handsome and he knew that he needed to marry young, to unite his poverty with that of another, if he was going to make a halfway bearable life for himself in their dust bowl of a town. None of the local women earned as much as a secretary for the local magistrate. And he also liked Antonia because she walked quickly, in long strides, without swaying her hips. She walked like a man.

Their marriage occurred against the better judgment and warnings of the magistrate and Doña Rita. They tried to make her see that this young man wasn't the last Coca-Cola in the desert. The magistrate advised her not to get pregnant, she could study in Córdoba if she wanted. Between the two of them they tried to get her to wait awhile, not to marry so hastily, to keep dating and get to know him better.

But his bull chest and golden cock were more persuasive and Antonia dove into the pit headfirst.

The first few months of their courtship went well, although Ricardo wasn't particularly talkative. It was as if he thought someone was going to charge him for every word he said. Sometimes Antonia wanted to tell him about her plans for the house, the places she'd like to go, what she wanted to call their future children. But Ricardo Camacho was hard as a river stone and there was no talking to him. And no leaving him either. Even on their wedding night they both knew they'd made a mistake but also that there was no going back. By the time they got married, Antonia was up to her neck in credit card debt. She bought all the materials for Ricardo to build a house on land that had belonged to his parents. That was the deal: she paid for the materials and he did the work. And so, when a bedroom, kitchen, and bathroom were complete they moved out to the edge of town. One big sandpit. Antonia learned of her pregnancy late; she hadn't been paying attention to the signs. She felt nothing, no nausea or dizziness. Nothing at all. Only by the third month did she realize that her period hadn't come in a while, so she went to the doctor during her lunch hour.

And now she had to tell Ricardo, which was the worst part because Ricardo had been very clear

about his need to be free and never tied down to any-
body or anyone. And he showed it every day. He got
up, had a coffee in the kitchen without sitting down,
rinsed out his mouth, and spat in the sink where they
did the dishes. Then he'd go out to work and didn't
come back until the evening, sometimes too drunk
to talk.

When she told her husband she was pregnant he
took it well. In fact, he almost seemed happy.

"I hope it's a boy, then he can help me at work,"
he said as enthusiastically as a man like him was able.

"So long as it's healthy, let God decide."

Ricardo's expression changed and the sneer returned. Before leaving for the bender of his life, he
said:

"What a surprise, contradicting me again..."

Irupé was born and Ricardo Camacho's bitterness grew more deep-rooted. He became difficult to
live with. Of the thirty days some months have, he
was in a foul mood for twenty-eight of them, and if
the month had twenty-eight days, he was drunk for
twenty. Cursing the spirits of the wind and water.
And after he'd first dared to lay a finger on Antonia,
he couldn't stop. He enjoyed slapping her around,
because he'd been working long hours, out of jealousy, because the girl was crying, or because River
had been relegated.

Five years after Irupé was born, Martincito arrived. And for a while Ricardo Charras seemed to mellow. But the peace barely lasted a day and when the boy started to cry every night, he resumed taking it out on his wife.

Antonia Charras wasted her twenties tossed around on the storm. For years she took the children to the office with her, with the magistrate's permission. She'd burst into Doña Rita's home at all hours with the children in her arms, upset and tearful, begging for sanctuary while Ricardo sobered up.

She aged two times faster than normal, getting doubly old and resentful, loving her children but also blaming them for keeping her there.

"Leave him, go live in the city, it'll do you good," Doña Rita would urge her. Antonia appeared to be in denial. He may have been a bad husband but he was a good father, and you can't have everything in life. It's hard enough to meet someone who works hard and doesn't beat the kids.

"I can't leave him. They're his children and he isn't bad with them. They have everything they need, he's bringing them up right and he's never raised his hand to them. I can't take them with me," Antonia would say.

"But does he love them?"

"I think so."

When the magistrate died of a painful but brief cancer that had stripped him down to the bone by the end, Antonia felt truly alone in the world. The magistrate was the only person Ricardo was afraid of. The first time he saw bruises on his secretary, he went straight out to find him and put her husband in his place with two or three bellowed epithets.

"Go to live with my wife," he said as he was dying. "Take the children and move into my home. Live there and keep her company when I'm gone."

But Antonia felt a failure for not being able to tame the man who had made her a sullen and fearful woman.

Martincito remembers his mother as he sits on the edge of the ditch alone with his dog. He thinks about how beautiful she seemed compared with the mothers of the kids at school. The time he spent watching her get ready before she went out to the courthouse. Her perfume and how sometimes he stole a little and dabbed it behind his ears, imitating her movements. When he starts to get sad he shakes his head the way his father taught him and realizes that it'll soon be time for "Where's that little shit got to?" But he needs more time; he has to gather his strength and brace himself, like when you have to lift something heavy and you let every cell of your body know to get ready. Which is why he brought his dog to the ditch before taking him home. He wanted to christen him with a childish pagan ritual, to give him the strength to ignore the brute Ricardo Camacho, the man who drove the women of the town crazy and who could lift three bags of cement on his shoulder, his father the circus freak. He wanted to take a moment to tell the dog that he just needed to be patient. It's easy for Martín. He works like a pack animal in spite of his tender years. It's when he's working that Ricardo feels he's brought someone useful into the world and lets him be.

He gets up, shakes the dust off his pants, and puts the dog in his bicycle basket, which he's lined with rags to make the journey home easier. When he arrives, Ricardo is about to take a shower and looks over his shoulder. The boy stops and holds out the dog like an offering.

"What's his name?"

"Don José."

"Bah, that name," he scoffs before getting undressed in the bathroom threshold, leaving his dirty clothes on the floor. "Irupé, hand me a towel."

Martín is frozen in the pose by the door, his hands still holding Don José out to the naked man, whose chest, stomach, and legs are covered in a curly mat of hair. A warm feeling of shame and love runs up Martín's legs. Irupé passes him with the towels and pets Don José. She knocks on the door, which opens at the pressure.

"Dad, the towel!"

"Put it in the sink!" her father shouts from the shower. They have an electric boiler that encourages haste when bathing. Irupé goes into the bathroom still looking at her brother and blindly puts the towel in the sink in a swift, skillful movement. Then she picks up her father's clothes and takes them to the laundry basket.

"Go out and sieve the sand and play with Don José so you can get to bed early," Irupé says to her little brother, and the boy goes out into the garden and starts to shovel sand over an old bedspring. He has strong arms and is skilled with his father's smallest shovel. The fine sand drops below. Don José sits still at his feet, staring out from the dark silences of his eyes. Back in the house, his sister continues with her chores, darning her father's socks the way her mother did during the years she lived with them.

That last winter—Martín had just turned six—Antonia spent all night up a tree in her nightdress and a sweater, having escaped her husband's fists and run until she found a tree she could climb and hide in. She swarmed up the nearest pepper tree as far as the branches would stand her weight. From her hiding place she looked down onto the little house they'd built by going into debt to half the town. The wood and zinc roofs, the metal frames, the laundry room with no hot water where the cold bit worst, the garden, which was always dry, as though the grass refused to grow for her. She spent the whole night clinging to the tree as hard as she could and cried and cried until the sun came up. As the cocks crowed and she felt her strength give out in the pepper tree, she knew that her body couldn't stand another beating. She went back to the house with this thought fresh in her mind. Ricardo was packing a bag with a change of clothes, his deodorant, and his ID.

"Where are you going?" she asked.

"To play football. The game's in San Javier, we'll spend the night there," he answered, putting on deodorant as though it were perfume.

"Will you be back tomorrow?"

"I don't know when I'll be back, Antonia. Don't be a pain in the ass."

"Fine."

Ricardo said goodbye to his children and left on the Fiorino that was his pride and joy. When night fell again and the children were asleep, Antonia packed the few clothes she had in a faded satchel, dug up her box of savings from the garden, put a little makeup in her handbag, and left the house it had taken her half a lifetime to build on tiptoe, with no tears or goodbyes. She got onto the first bus leaving town that didn't go anywhere near San Javier because she didn't want to run even the slightest chance of crossing paths with Ricardo. She went from one town to another farther away, and that was all anyone knew. The next day the children woke up and called for her before going out to look. Ricardo came back three days later and found them in Doña Rita's house.

Antonia had left the book of her life open for anyone to write what they liked inside. She went without even leaving a farewell letter on the table, and they never heard from her again. Doña Rita searched for her as best she could, asking acquaintances in other towns if they'd seen her, but never heard anything. Nobody reported her as missing, voluntarily or otherwise.

He told people his own story. He claimed she'd left with someone else, making himself the cuckolded victim. The idiots in town believed the abandoned husband's version and were sorry for the children. Girlfriends weren't in short supply, and some even tried to make friends with Irupé and Martín, but sooner or later his tantrums sent them running and now the only witnesses to his nightly drunkenness, his dinners of greasy pork chops and six fried eggs in front of the evening's seedy talk shows, were his children.

Right now, Ricardo Camacho is lost in his reverie of an abandoned man, leaning his elbows on the table after dinner with a carton of white wine, giving his liver the brew it so loves, burping out the soda he mixes it with, watching Irupé do the dishes. She has to stand on a cinder block to reach the sink comfortably. Watching Martín finish sifting the sand while the dog that won't be good for anything not now or ever gets between his feet.

"Just give the mutt a kick to the head if it's bothering you!" he shouts at the boy.

"He won't kick a puppy, you can't do that," Irupé answers.

"The dog is the most treacherous animal in the world, after your mother."

Martín bags up all the sifted sand and then starts to make a bed for Don José out of an apple box and rags. He knows that later that night, when his father has passed out from the booze, he'll take him inside to sleep in his bed. He shares a room with Irupé and knows she won't say anything. Once the bed is made and he's put the dog inside (God forbid he starts whining), Martincito goes to sit at the table to eat the milanesa with buttered spaghetti and cheese his sister made for them both. They eat in silence, but under the table Irupé kicks his feet, telling her little brother not to worry, she's there.

Soon Ricardo gets loquacious.

"How long have you been friends with Doña Rita?"

"Since Mommy was here...I can't remember."

"Since Mommy was alive. That's the right way to say it."

"Dad!" Irupé interrupts. "Don't say that!"

"I'll say what I like. That's what happened, isn't it? Your mother's dead, isn't she?"

"No, she isn't dead. She just left," says Martín, tearfully eating his dinner.

"So, if that fuckinwhore, which is what she is, if that motherfucking whore came back tomorrow, you'd just welcome her with open arms?"

"We don't know what's going to happen," Irupé answers.

"Nothing, nothing will happen because that fuckinwhore isn't coming back, got it?"

The two children are silent. Ricardo tries again.

"Got it?"

"Yes, Daddy."

"Yes, Daddy. May I be excused?" Martín asks.

"No. Stay here. You can go to bed if you like," he says to Irupé.

Irupé gathers the plates, washes them, wipes down the table with a damp cloth, and goes to bed like a little slave retiring to her quarters.

"Don't keep the boy up late, he's tired from having to sieve all that sand."

"When I was his age, I could sift five wheelbarrows of sand and I didn't make a fuss about it."

Martín doesn't say anything; his head remains bowed.

"You've brought that dog into my home and I know that it was you who told the old woman to come fill up my head with her nonsense. You should be playing with boys, hunting pigeons with your slingshot, not visiting an old fuckinwhore who has you twisted around her little finger. It seems as though I'm a bad father and your mother is a saint."

Ricardo gets up and goes outside to take a piss, staring out at the street, saying, Here I am, world, this fat, musty cock is mine, this stinking yellow urine is mine and I own this house, these children, this sky and this night. He knows that no one will come by because they live in the ass-end of the town. The street didn't even have a name until a couple of years ago when they called it Pasaje La Piedad. But pity is a virtue in scarce supply around here. There are only the lives of children crying in secret for their mother. Children woken in the middle of the night by the cries of their father's short-lived lovers as they fuck with hurried urgency. In the dust bowl from which Antonia escaped, all that's left are the children's shriveled hearts. Pity is long gone.

He shakes out his dick, wipes his hands on his pants, and sits back down at the table opposite his son, who hasn't moved a muscle.

"Do you know why your mother left?"

Martín shakes his head.

"Because of you. Because you didn't want a little brother. Did you know that?"

The boy remains silent. Outside, the dog begins to whine.

"Go shut that dog up."

Martín goes out to the bed and picks the dog up. He stands outside, on the other side of the plastic strips tied back with a cloth, taking a protective stance, thinking that if his father tries to do something to Don José he can escape into the bush. His father would never find him at night. He has loads of secret hiding places. The bush is his friend.

"I'm not going to do anything to the dog. But I do want to make sure you know it was your fault your mother left. Spoiled little brat. Your sister wanted a little brother; look at you. You didn't want any other boys at home. You faggot."

"I didn't say that to Mommy."

"Yes, you did. She told me that you told her you didn't want any little brothers or sisters. So she felt sick at the end because she was taking contraceptives."

His tongue feels thick in his mouth. The syrupy alcohol has begun to slosh around his brain.

"But around here, the bastard is always me...always me...and the only thing this chump does is work so you can go complain about your father to that old woman. Making friends with that old woman and making me look like a fool."

Irupé calls from the bedroom:

"Let Martín come to bed. It's late, Dad."

Ricardo looks at him and barks: "Leave the dog and go to bed...or take his cot inside and put it next to your bed. But make sure he doesn't piss on anything, or you'll both have hell to pay."

Martín picks up the bed too. As he passes his father, he stops for a moment.

"Good night, Daddy. Bless me."

Ricardo makes a cross over his forehead.

"God bless you. 'Night."

Martín goes out through the curtain hanging where a door should be, into his bedroom.

Buzzing already, Ricardo Camacho picks up the scissors and cuts the corner off another carton of wine. Number two down the hatch! He sits there until his head bangs down on the table, waking him up. He has no idea what time it is and he's left his watch in the bedroom.

He goes out to piss in the garden again, spraying everywhere. Again, he wipes his hands on his pants. Swaying and swearing under his breath, he goes into his children's bedroom. Irupé is sleeping covered in a blanket that used to belong to her grandmother to keep out the cold. The boy has his back to the door and the dog's cot is at the foot of the bed. He sleeps in his underwear. At one point he turns over and moans up at the ceiling as though he were crying in his sleep. Ricardo stares at his children, still swaying in the threshold, holding on to the doorframe, sickened by the smell of damp from the unventilated bathroom. Urine is still dripping from his dick but he hasn't noticed. His pants get wet. He goes into the room, pulls the blanket over Irupé, and strokes her hair, which is just like Antonia's. He's feeling dizzy; the room is shrinking and expanding just to spite him. He grabs the end of his daughter's bed to steady himself for a moment. In the silence, he feels a complete stranger in this room. Not just in his children's bedroom but in their lives too. As though he weren't their father. Martín has stopped moaning and his eyelids shudder as his eyeballs skate around beneath them. He goes over to his bed to cover him with the sheet. He stands watching him sleep for a long time and in the end bends over, supporting himself on the headboard, and gives him a long kiss on the mouth. Then he lurches unsteadily back upright and goes to bed.

To Martín, it feels like a satsuma segment pressed against his lips. The words "Sleeping Beauty" run through his head. He turns to look at his sister and sees her sitting up in bed. She has the bare lamp in her hand, ready to smash over Ricardo Camacho's head if he lingered a moment longer than he did. Martín moves into her bed and they sleep together. When Don José whines, later that night, they bring him into the bed too.

THE NIGHT DOESN'T WANT TO END JUST YET

A good sushi recipe calls for a special kind of rice available in most supermarkets: short-grained, white, and soft with plenty of starch so as to give an extremely sticky consistency to each bite. A variety similar to the Italian carnaroli and arborio, which are used for risotto. Once cooked, the grains gleam and have a lovely firm texture and good flavor. But really, for poor travestis any rice will do. The same goes for the vinegar and even the cheese, although they don't mix rice with cheese in Asia.

Vienen por mí (They're Coming for Me),
Claudia Rodríguez

Whenever my personal finances allow, I make scones and invite my friends to tea. I'm a humble travesti with something of the English lady about me. I always follow the same recipe as my mother. She got it from her mother, who inherited it in turn from her grandmother. My mother would sell them in town. People greedily snatched them out of her hands.

"The most important thing to remember when you make scones is not to knead the dough and to have cold hands," she'd say.

Inviting my friends to tea is my little luxury, the luxury of the poor travesti, Claudia Rodríguez would say. "Any old rice is good enough for the poor travesti…" Mine come out exactly like my mother's because it's the same recipe and she shared the secrets to making good scones with me, just casually, like she didn't give it a second thought, while I helped her in the kitchen. "This is my living legacy." So, whenever I have a few pesos to spare and want to give myself a treat, I make scones.

Sometimes I get on a roll. Some nights, I hop from one john's car into another and my handbag fills up with bills. If another john, or a mugger, doesn't steal them from me, I make enough to reward myself. I buy a lovely package of loose tea at Las Mil Grullas, and a red fruit jam, and light up the travisignal to invite my friends to afternoon tea. They like my scones, or so they say. They never turn them down, at least.

But nights when my luck's in are few and far between; the rest are depressing and repetitive and on them I barely make enough for a quarter kilo of brown bread. Some times of the year, the life of a prostitute weighs down on you like a sack of rubble.

There I was, on my balcony overlooking Calle
Mendoza, a travesti Juliet, an Eva Perón pontificat-
ing to a nonexistent crowd, on a balcony (oh my, if
it could talk) in dark tights, red boots, and a puffer
jacket that barely covered my ass. It was very cold.
An ideal night for throwing in the towel, but I held
out, because you get used to holding out. Not out of
any special feeling. Not a single mark had stopped by
all night; not many people come down this street in
the yellowy lamplight. Earlier, in the building opposite that blocks out my sun, there was a party. Now,
at three in the morning, the street was dead.

I saw a car coming from a couple of blocks away.
Something akin to hope scuttled up my legs. Every
far-off car is a potential customer. Oh, I hope it's
a customer, I hope it's a customer. The car looked
new and it was heading my way. It still needed not
to turn at 9 de Julio, I yearned for it to come to me,
to the little ground-floor balcony that acts as my
Amsterdam shop window. The car continued and
didn't turn at 9 de Julio. In fact, it looked as if it was
slowing down. Yes, it was going slow. A shiny new
Peugeot 307. Inside were four well-built men about
twenty-five years old. The kind of handsome kids
you really relish screwing over. They stopped at my
balcony.

One stuck his head out of the window.

"Will you give us a present?"

"I don't give presents."

"My friend's going to Italy and we want him to leave with a nice memory."

"But you need to pay for presents."

I turned around to show them my lovely Serrana ass.

"How much?"

I gave them a price based on their skin and clothes.

"Not if you were made of gold," he answered.

I shrugged and looked away. Ignoring them. A man on a bicycle passed by, on the other side of the car. He looked at me and I looked back. The man held my gaze in spite of the company. I'd serviced him before; he was just leaving work at the gas station on Colón and Neuquén, about six blocks away.

"You're dumping us that easily?" asked another of the kids from inside the car.

The man on the bicycle backed off and rode away slowly. The guys in the car seemed jealous. They conferred among themselves and eventually one of them said, "Well, we won't waste any more of your time." They pulled away. I could hear laughter from inside the car.

I waited for the guy on the bicycle to come back, he was a good customer. But he didn't.

Fifteen minutes later, the guys who wanted the freebie came back. They began to whine, claiming not to have any money, even though their car, clothes, accents, skin, and watches said otherwise.

"We're taking you to a country club," the driver shouted. "That ought to be enough."

Enough for what, I wondered. I couldn't pay my rent with stories about going to a country club. Eventually, after plenty of to-ing and fro-ing, haggling like we were in a market, we reached an agreement that seemed fair to me. At that hour you're supposed to take what you can get, not look a gift horse in the mouth, even if it is just ten pesos. When you've failed as a whore, start begging, you don't have a choice. And these well-fed guys were handsome. If we were in a club and I wasn't on the clock I'd sleep with all of them without charging a cent. Before going out, I spritzed on a little perfume and tucked some makeup into my bag, just in case the horseplay messed up my look. I sat in the front, on the lap of a guy with legs like tree trunks, the one who'd said, "Not if you were made of gold." He immediately poked his mound into the black hole between my butt cheeks and started rubbing.

"Watch out she doesn't scratch you with her whiskers," said one of the guys behind.

"Hey, be nice to my girlfriend," said the driver.

I was already regretting having gotten into the car. They were listening to *cuarteto* at full volume. It was hot because they had the heating on. I could feel sweat dripping down my cheeks, my back was damp, and I was wondering what kind of butcher would be required to handle flesh like this. Where was she when I needed her? I searched deep inside but she wasn't there. All that was there were the travesti who needed money to pay some of the back rent she owed and the horny cow ready to fuck daddy's boys in a country club. Behind us, one of them took off his T-shirt to reveal a set of abs that rippled like cobblestones.

"Look what you'll be having for dinner. You like? We're rugby players."

"From which club?"

"Don't tell her," said the one driving.

From my vantage point atop the brick shithouse shoving his cock in my ass with undue aggression, I didn't have a good view of the body on display. All four were wearing a lot of cologne and I began to feel nauseous. It was like dunking your head in a bucket of air freshener. I was horrified to think that I might never get it out of my nostrils.

They were driving fast and talking nonstop, laughing heartily, forcing me to grope them in the car. They asked the best endowed of the four to show me the treat he kept in his pants. They claimed to be friends with a lot of famous people, saying they knew Flor de la V, Pachi, María Laura, but none of their boasts rang true. They honked the horn at passersby to startle them. They swerved close to motorcyclists, shouted insults at the garbagemen on Caraffa Avenue. They zigzagged up the highway, singing songs, "My hands wrote the letter and my fingers set the trap." I gulped and thought about how I really wasn't all that dedicated to the job, how I didn't go out regularly. I scolded myself for not earning enough money, for turning down johns because I didn't like them, for going to bed when I was tired. All that fuss about going out to work and then, without fail, a point came in the month when things started to get antsy and I had to take gigs like this one. To sit in a car with idiots like these, going somewhere I'd never been to do who knows what.

It was three-thirty in the morning by the time we got to the house in the country club. I still thought I could handle the situation, that I was thinking clearly. I'd made sure to clock the way we'd come in and the way back out again. I was strong and sober. There was nothing these stupid rich kids could do to me. The entrance was ajar and loud electronic music seeped out. There weren't any neighbors. Inside the house were four other guys, more rugby players to judge by the size of them. Every horny city girl's dream. All my faggot friends' dream and mine too, a little. A gang bang with pretty boys. The only female in a tribe of orangutans in Gola shoes and Key Biscayne T-shirts. In the living room sat a sculpture of an old motorcycle on top of a low table made from old, dark wood. It was a strange house. High ceilings, enormous heavy doors, and stone walls. They told me why it looked so unusual; it had once been a church. Now that it was a house, all its sacredness, all the holy spirits that still lurked inside had died with me. My simple presence was enough to profane whatever prayers still hung in the air. But they wanted to keep the atmosphere going. They talked about what the property was worth, the wood in the lintels, how old the chañar tree at the entrance was. On the living room table was a swathe of drugs of all kinds; whatever drugs you can think of lay before me. Some of them were walking around in boxer shorts because it was hot inside.

"The house has underfloor heating," said the one who drove the car, who was apparently the owner.

They offered me whatever I wanted from the table.

"I want cocaine," I told him. I wasn't about to lose my head.

"It's dragonfly dust, try some," said the owner.

I did and it was smooth, like water. Ever since I moved to Córdoba I'd been in close proximity to churches and religious schools. Now I was taking drugs in a former church surrounded by rhinoceros-scale bodies covered in bruises and scars, snorting dragonfly cocaine and waiting to do my thing. Two of them complained: they'd brought a travesti instead of a woman. She hadn't had surgery. Her nose was ugly. "Look at those tits. No. Thank you, but no." So the group to be served was reduced to six impatient, high young men trying to act like bad boys. They took me into one of the bedrooms, Mommy and Daddy's room, the master bedroom.

"I only have water to offer you. I doubt you'd like what we're drinking, my dad's wine."

I didn't know what to say to that, so I just shrugged and followed him into the bedroom. He told me that the bed, or the room, I can't remember which, could spin around, following the sun.

Round one was with three of them. Two who weren't in the car, and the one concerned about my whiskers. They were so far gone they could barely keep their balance. They struggled to wield their skinny little cocks, which might have looked very pretty but weren't good for anything, and it all devolved into groping and licking. Very professionally performed, of course. I noticed that whisker boy took advantage of the tangle of flesh to stroke the rock-hard ass of his partner in the quartet. I was straddled over one of them, trying to get a cock the consistency of drying mortar hard, and through the corner of my eye I saw the kid casually reaching for my cock, the cock underneath me, and the cock next to me. At one point he climbed over his friend, pretending to be trying to give me a kiss, but then he faked a stumble over the one underneath me and slipped his tongue along his neck. I couldn't work like that.

"What's wrong, man? Are you trying to steal my job? And in that guy's parents' bed? No one told me that I'd be sharing it with another actress."

Which is how you expose a sneak.

The one underneath me sat up, wiping his neck, saying, "Sick, you licked me, you son of a bitch!"

I enjoyed having given him away.

The opportunist didn't say a word. He pretended to be wasted. He was faking, I know it; he wasn't that far gone when I arrived, and he hadn't had time to get so drunk. The other one got up in disgust. Suddenly he was sober.

"You're impossible, it's always the same with you, you bastard," he said to the groper, and walked naked out into the hall. Meanwhile, the one who had gotten licked got up too and shook him, pushing him off the bed.

"Get out of here. You can come back on your own later."

The groper acted all offended, outraged that they believed a tranny's word over his. He pulled on his boxers and left, leaning on the walls. The one who stayed with me eventually gave up trying to get an erection. *They won't be able to get it up for the rest of their lives*, I thought maliciously. *Let their cocks never get hard ever again.* I put the curse on them, concentrating hard to make it come true. Stammering, stone drunk, he told me I was ugly, I didn't turn him on, I didn't work on his erection hard enough. Even with the doors closed, the electronic music was deafening. The owner of the house brought in a dildo. He pushed the impotent guy with the bull's haunches off the bed and he immediately passed out on the floor. The new guy seemed a little less of an idiot than the others. A lovely brunette with freckles and green eyes. His pupils were enormous. I guessed that the dildo belonged to his mother, because it came out of the bathroom. He asked me to penetrate him with it. With a shiny black cock his mother must have used to jerk off with too. I became multitudes, I didn't have hands but tentacles, a thousand mouths,

I was all the prostitutes there ever were in one bed. I gave him a blow job while I penetrated him with his mother's dildo and stroked his balls like you'd stroke a puppy's head. I was a one-whore orchestra. Fortunately, he did have a lovely erection and things got a little more fun. I wasn't thinking so much about how to be rid of them and out of this uncomfortable situation. Outside, as the music went boom, boom, boom, we could hear laughter. As usual, I assumed they were laughing at me.

The next round was with the guy whose lap I'd sat on in the car. I was finally introduced to the cock that had harassed me all through the journey. It wasn't especially remarkable but it smelled good and it was bright and golden. The image of Erendira scrubbing the sheets stained with her customers' sweat came to mind. Through the window, the others were watching and filming. I took the goldfish out of my mouth and stepped back.

"Why didn't you tell me you were going to film this?"

The guy in the bed didn't react. From outside, the owner called out, asking how much to film me. I doubled the price and they agreed. What did it matter. When the deed was done, the pack of hyenas broke up. I got dressed in the revolving room and promised myself I wouldn't take another risk like that again.

Never again. When I came out of the bedroom, the guys were waiting for me, only now they were joined by three or four girls who'd arrived while I was performing like a third-world porn star.

"You can't actually pay this tramp," said one of the girls, snorting the same dragonfly dust I had.

The owner told me that he couldn't take me back to the boardinghouse, and seeing as I didn't see to all of them, they wouldn't be paying the price we'd agreed on. They didn't have as much money as they thought.

"And you need to wash my sister's dress, she puked herself, the idiot."

They all laughed their shitty laugh. I fumbled with my boots in silence. They turned up the music and started jumping around and dancing. One of them leapt like an ape in front of me, screaming, I guess, the kind of scream that rugby players let out before a match. Meanwhile, I was trying to pull up the zip on my boot, which was too small for my foot. I stood up with dignity and left in silence through the old door of their fucking church, taking a bottle of vodka with me. They might have been rich but it was a brand you could buy in the supermarket. I walked down the cobbled streets and out through the entrance to the country club. The guard waved with a yellow smile that warmed my heart. The night didn't want to end just yet. I got a ride back to the center in a baker's delivery van, paying for the trip with a conscientious blow job, luxuriating in the aromas of recently baked buns and croissants.

When I got back to the boardinghouse, I put a very expensive-looking watch that I'd found by the side of the bed, underneath one of the embroidered pillows, on the nightstand. I'd tucked it into my panties. It was like ice. In the morning I went to the Planeta Gallery and sold it at the price the buyer offered. I didn't even haggle. It was a lot of money to me. I wasn't worried about them coming back to the boardinghouse looking for it. People don't usually complain about my thefts or report them. I guess their reputation is worth more to them. I did some sums, working out what was left over after paying a few months' rent, and decided that it was a good night after all. I got all the things I needed to make scones and put some money on my cell phone. I sent a text message to my friends: *This afternoon, tea with scones at home.*

The other secret to making sure your scones are light and rise properly is to leave the dough to cool in the refrigerator for at least an hour. It never fails. Leave the dough in the fridge and don't knead, just stir.

I'M A FOOL
TO WANT YOU

She was a beauty. You might ask how a haggard, old, toothless, alcoholic junkie slut could be a beauty. Oh, I'd reply...old sluts like that, we've seen plenty. And we've seen plenty of beautiful ladies too, of course, thousands of them, but none were as beautiful as Billie. A pair of girls like us, you know, special ladies, like we used to say to the boys who asked what we kept in our panties, girls at night, shy fags by day, didn't get to meet many other kinds. Old toothless whores, warm and spicy as a chili pepper, were our friends, part of our everyday routine. We embraced them, giving them free haircuts and makeovers, tending lovingly to their hearts, hair, and asses. We waited until the last paying customer had left the beauty salon and let in the vulnerable: single mothers, widows who needed our skilled hands for a moment of beauty. It didn't matter how tired my friend and I, whom you might describe as the stars of this story, were. After that we'd close up (the owner trusted us with the keys) like nothing had happened.

We always had enough energy and willpower to aid these dissolute women in their struggles against ugliness and neglect. We didn't meet many respectable people, thank the Blessed Virgin of Guadalupe. It's not as though we were so far from respectability ourselves. Deep down we were naive young things; our sins didn't cast a shadow over our innocence. But it wasn't our lot to meet respectable men and women. Disciplined, God-fearing folk didn't cross our paths. To escape poverty, respectable women obeyed all the rules and put up with the beatings and familial strife that came their way. Sometimes we'd do their hair and their scalps would reek of the ammonium smell that came with refusing to let go of the genuine pearl necklaces that hung from their necks like shackles. The Goldmans, the Stuarts, the Yorks, these women were terribly boring and on the few occasions we did meet them they eyed us with extreme wariness. As we did their hair, they clutched their purses to their gaunt chests as if they were afraid we'd grab something. Sometimes I felt like saying: "Listen, lady, the only thing I'm liable to steal of yours is your husband."

Then I'd remember how ugly these men were and my anger would fade. It's just that they're afraid of you for no good reason. Especially these old women. No, that's not true, I won't lie, the truth is that everyone is either afraid of us or hates us. You can't claim that hatred is the sole domain of the society ladies of New York; of course not. The hatred people feel for us is a legacy of humanity.

Billie, on the other hand, wasn't scared of us at all. She was a sweetheart. A real sweetheart. When I think about it, she was the true society lady. She'd call us "darling," "honey," "love," and "babe." It was enough to bring us to tears.

Ava's the other star of this story. My friend, my sister, my fellow keeper of the scissors and curlers (she named herself after Ava Gardner, as I'm sure you've already guessed). We met the same way we later met Billie. In a smoking den in Harlem, one night in the New York winter. Our maidens' eyes lit up the moment we saw one another and we've been inseparable ever since. Ava always cried when Billie stroked her hair and spoke to her in her scratchy voice, with her breath stinking of alcohol and cigarettes, telling her that everything would be all right one day, honey, the world would change, darling. It was crazy; she said it with such conviction that it sounded true. Like us, she knew just how much the world needed to change, how much there was to do, how much needed to be turned upside down. It wasn't going to happen overnight. But she lied to cheer us up and it was better than love.

How did we meet? It's one of those things that makes you feel as though you have a purpose, something just for you, like fingerprints. Our destiny, Ava would say, we were destined to meet her. Even though we were a pair of *chilangas*, we visited Harlem regularly. We liked to go at night or when it started to get dark because your beard didn't show so much underneath the makeup and also because at the smoking dens you'd find black men with packages between their legs worth thousands and thousands of carats. You'd think about the treasure to be found in a black man's package, the rubies, emeralds, and pearls that burst out when they unzipped their pants like a chest, a coffer with seven locks, and, well . . . I don't want to be crude; you don't need me to tell you exactly what it was we went to find in Harlem.

Ava and I had learned that men's wariness when it came to fags and travestis melted away when they smoked marijuana or drank too much rum. They'd all say, no, no, no, never with a travesti, until it got to three or four in morning and all the women had left with white men. Then, lo and behold, they would make an almost imperceptible gesture that only we understood to follow them down some alley, or take them back to our place.

Oh yes, we brought black men with lavish treasures back to our part of the two-story house we rented from a woman who spoiled us, Mamma Mercy, whom we loved deeply. She was a black woman of impressive size who was missing the index finger on her left hand. She'd cut it off by accident one Halloween, carving pumpkins for a rich family in Manhattan. They threw her out of the house with her hand wrapped in a handkerchief that barely stemmed the bleeding and her finger in a paper bag and never opened the door to her again. She decided to move into the ground floor of her home and rent out the top one to young ladies. But she was unlucky with her young ladies: they tended to slip away in the middle of the night owing several months' rent. Mamma Mercy was a generous woman and never resorted to brute force or hiring thugs to collect the money owed to her, so she was always being swindled by one person or another, the dope. Ava and I came to her door having seen an advertisement in the drugstore. We told her that we worked as beauticians at a salon in Manhattan, she let us in, and we immediately felt at home.

"A pair of fags loose in New York!" she cried on the day we moved into the upstairs apartment, which had its own bathroom and bathtub and windows that looked out onto a courtyard presided over by a chestnut tree.

Oh, Mamma Mercy! I'd bet my indigenous eyes you never ate better stews than hers.

In the romantic sphere, Ava always had more luck than me. People thought she was stupid because she barely said a word and you always had to say her name two or three times to get her attention. I thought she was pretty slow myself at first, poor thing. A lovely, silent faggot, who was always apologizing or asking permission with long, elegant fingers that looked like knitting needles. Later I realized that she wasn't stupid at all. She'd learned to separate herself from this world and take refuge in a palatial one of her own. The only thing that kept her tied to earthly affairs was her beauty. Generations of Teutonic blood had bequeathed her with the bluest eyes in the world, which assured her a healthy stream of lovers. A travesti like that, with eyes of the deepest blue and skin whiter than milk, had it made when it came to men.

"Come over here, *güerita*," cooed the Latinos in the street, almost licking her ears, but she paid no attention; she was strolling through the halls and ballrooms of her mind.

I'm short with a round waist, because I always had a weakness for pastries, and still do. My only virtue as a travesti is I'm almost entirely hairless. From my indigenous heritage, I suppose. But I've never been much of a beauty. And men had no trouble telling me so.

Sometimes, I'd pretend to be asleep after coming back from the smoking dens in Harlem, a lonely little bitch. Ava would come in with a man with gleaming black skin, maybe six foot five, six foot, and put out a wooden screen for privacy. Our wigs (made with real hair of course) sat on the chest of drawers on top of mannequin heads, and our dresses were hidden underneath the bed. Sometimes, the guy in question would realize that there was someone on the other side of the screen, because I'd coughed or rolled around in the scratchy sheets. Mostly, they were so drunk I could have been pounding on a typewriter for all they cared. But sometimes, the guy who'd realized I was there would lose stiffness in his treasure and say:

"Who's there?"

"My sister," she'd reply.

"Why don't you wake her up to come join us?"

"She's asleep, leave her alone," Ava would say. She was always stingy with her men, she never shared.

And when the guy took off his shirt, I breathed in all the secrets impregnated in the skin, a more delicious chocolate even than the one made by my grandmother, who was more like my mother, may she rest in peace. When Ava ripped off those pants so very quickly, I could also breathe in the smells from down below. Ava was very clean. She'd take him to the chest of drawers where the wigs were, cup some water from a can, and rub the man's balls with a little soap, making a foam that woke up his chest of rubies and doubloons, which grew and grew until it was a sword. Then she swallowed it whole. Like a fakir, without a blink or a wince. And when they plunged inside her in bed she'd ask them please, not to make her cry out.

And when she said that, they just pushed harder and she didn't mind the pain. I felt my groin, which was no kind of treasure at all, grow harder and harder and I hated myself for it, because I hated my dick almost as much as I hated myself.

But that was before, before Billie. Before I met her, I had those feelings inside of me. When I went to pee, I'd look down between my legs and think: I hate you, I hate you so much, my sadness is because of you. I hate you so much I ought to cut you off with a pair of secateurs. Now I don't treat it that way. Now, sometimes, when I take off my clothes and look down at my dangling cock, I even say I love you, I forgive you, I didn't mean what I said.

Did I tell you my name? No, I didn't. My name is Maria, like my grandmother. Really, she was always my mother, because she was the woman who raised me and took me by the hand to go see the end-of-year fireworks thirty blocks from the Zócalo in Colonia San Rafael, where I grew up. My mother married a gringo when I was twelve and went off to live in California, promising to come back for me the following year, but we never saw her again. I lived with my grandmother until I was seventeen. One day, I brought her breakfast in bed but she'd passed away, with that beatific expression on her face that people who pass away in their sleep get. It was a very just death, I thought. And the thought was such consolation that I didn't shed a tear.

With nothing left to tie me to Mexico, I sold the little we had. I had one-peso flings with every good man I came across until I had enough money for the plane ticket and ended up in New York, working as an apprentice hairdresser in the salons of Harlem.

My first great mentor was a Puerto Rican fag we called Toucan because of his enormous hooked nose and because he flapped his arms around the heads of his customers like a hysterical bird. He had an elegant, select clientele, a club of coquettish ladies who would only have their hair cut by a queen like him.

"You can style like the gods. You can do the hair of a movie star, make any of them look pretty. But you learn to be a coiffeur with black women's hair," he'd say. "You need to straighten hair like that, curls so rebellious they bring tears to your eyes. You truly learn the art of hairdressing curling black hair, because working with it, thick and oh so tangled, is like working with the impossible things of this world."

Toucan didn't just teach me to be a good hairdresser. He taught me to earn my customers' affection with my wiles, doing my dance around their sparse hairdos like a plumed serpent. He taught me to earn good tips and survive in New York, always smiling, always nice to *tutto il mondo*. He showed me how to be a fag in the country of gringos and not die in the attempt. When I think about it, I get emotional. The depressing bowing to everyone so they wouldn't kill me, hours bleeding in a corner somewhere after a beating, the pain of a Latino here, in the promised land...you can imagine, but it's not like how you imagine. It's all part of a past that's over now, I tell myself. It lies dead, deep somewhere in my heart. And then came life in Mamma Mercy's house, life with Ava, and life with Billie.

Because I'm Latina, the black men didn't pay me so much attention in the light of day. And because I was dressed as an ordinary man, they just saw me as one of them. Blacks and Latinos went through the same shit back then. We had to hide and protect each other like a brotherhood, which is why I think they didn't take much notice of me. Not my skin, features, or the Guadalajaran eyes I inherited from my saintly grandmother. The blacks wanted to travel, get to know different skins, see how their skin contrasted with the *güeras*. Which is why I didn't have as much luck as Ava.

Poor little Mary, no love and no tenderness, let's put her on the street, her life's such a mess...

The smoking dens were always a little slice of heaven. They had all the wild, endangered fauna you could hope to meet, people you didn't see in the street, or the jazz bars, and especially not in the light of day. Blacks, travestis, whores, fags, men who'd lost legs and arms after the war, elephantine fat women, dwarves, Asians. It made you feel at home. Of all their qualities, the best was that there it was the whites who were out of place. For the first time in their lives, they acted with respect. In the smoking dens, they didn't think they were better than anyone the way they did the rest of the time. Nothing belonged to the whites in the Harlem smoking dens;

they were terrified that a black man was going to crack their skull. Occasionally you'd see one leave with a slash across their face, or their pockets empty. Snobs have always existed and here was no exception. White writers, Broadway actresses, and a few politicians went to Harlem to listen to jazz and get lost in our hell with nothing to orient them up in the sky or down below.

There's no point in lying; we didn't really like jazz much. It's so *boring*, darling! Basically, we were pretty stupid. Music you couldn't hum along to, baraddabaddabapapapa, trumpets that gave you a headache. No, it wasn't the right music for us, or at least not for me. I'd grown up with rancheras, corridos, and boleros. Music from warm climes. But we liked the black men who played the instruments and the black gangsters who went to listen to the devil's music every night. Tararara, baddabaddaboo, papapapdeedeedeedoo. Then we met her and the music that had seemed so strange and hard to sing grew familiar; it sounded just as lovely as the songs my grandmother sang as she ground coffee. And we liked it. Not all jazz, but definitely hers.

One night, Ava and I went to a den on the top floor of a house in the center of Harlem. It was the first time we'd been there. We were drunk on moonshine bourbon, the best way to recover from a hangover that had kept us in bed all day. Not knowing the place had made us shy, and because we were shy we needed a drink. It was just an unfurnished apartment with one bathroom for men and women and the windows covered with heavy curtains made from coarse material. We lay back on a dilapidated sofa, in a pair of very old dresses with seams bursting at the back and waist. We clumsily made an effort to latch on to a conversation between a pair of whores nearby. One was telling the other about how she'd accidentally bitten Frank Sinatra's cock and he'd just slapped her without a word. The gossip was interrupted by a commotion on the stairs. We thought it was the cops, that we were finally going to get pinched. And you know what happens when the cops arrest a couple of girls like us. Ava toasted me and downed her glass of whiskey.

"I've had a good life with you, sister."

I hugged her but I couldn't return the sentiment. I thought that life had been shit and the world was shit but I didn't say anything because I didn't want to ruin the solemn moment. Suddenly we heard a cackle from someone whose voice was strangely familiar. *Next there'll be shooting*, I thought, but no. Instead, we heard a very, very tired voice, extremely gentle, like the clinking of rusted cans, climbing up the stairs. First came Louis Armstrong, Louis Armstrong himself, ladies and gentlemen, and behind him a lady, it's the only way to describe her, a lady in a white satin dress embroidered with little stones that glittered brighter than all the packages wandering around that evening.

It was Billie Holiday.

When she got to the last step, her heel got tangled up in the train of her beautiful dress, or maybe the fur coat she was wearing, which she dragged along the floor as if it wasn't worth anything, and she fell over. I, in my antiquated, torn dress, leapt up, and, I don't know how, I transported myself over there and caught her in my arms before she hit the floor. It was as though a spell had been cast to freeze everyone else; even Armstrong was just standing there, looking dumbfounded.

Grabbing hold of me, her hands groped at my head, knocking my wig askew, pulling it down over my forehead and exposing my receding hairline, *Oh! My receding male hairline!* People started to laugh.

"What's the matter? Did the spell get broken?"

"Cinderella's become a man!"

Mockery was coming from all sides; everyone was digging in the knife.

"Enough!" I pleaded. "Stop it!"

Ava ran over to help me with my wig and Billie Holiday stared at them all with a hatred so concentrated that it was as though steam were coming out of her eyes.

"Listen up, you pieces of shit. If anyone laughs at this woman again, they'll be going home without their balls," she barked.

Armstrong laughed again and struck up a conversation with the gossipy prostitutes while Billie Holiday stroked my cheek, saying: "Thank you, darling." She came over to sit on the sofa with Ava and me. She had a little leather bag in her coat pocket full of fragrant marijuana, more fragrant even than her, and started to roll a joint for us to share. When she was done, she called out:

"Hey! Bupa! A light!"

Armstrong came over with a lighter that must have been worth more than my whole life and lit the joint in my mouth like a real gentleman, the sweetest gesture a man had ever shown me in a place like that.

"Ladies," he said, taking off his hat.

"Let me introduce you to my friends, this is..."

"Ava," said my friend, her panties all in a twist.

"Maria," said I, holding out my hand to shake, but he took it and kissed it instead.

And I swear by the light inside me that neither Ava nor I, ordinarily great connoisseurs of the treasure to be found in underwear, checked out his package. We were dazzled, I don't know, his smile, his voice, his hat. We were sitting with Billie Holiday, and Armstrong himself had lit a joint for me. Someone with power, refinement, and prestige had stepped in to preserve my dignity.

Holiday stayed with us all night, asking where we lived, what kind of food we liked, whether we were full-time travestis (I can't remember if those were her exact words). She asked us about our shoe sizes, whether we liked her marijuana, if we had any of her records, if we'd ever heard her sing, if we wanted to have dinner with her, if we could do her hair for one of her concerts, if we liked jazz, where we'd gotten our dresses, how it was possible to have such poor taste, our dresses were horrible, she had a lot of dresses she didn't wear anymore, she'd give them to us so we didn't have to wear moth-eaten old rags. She laughed, got emotional, drank until she couldn't drink another drop, went on laughing, and fell asleep in my lap. Her cheeks were sunken beneath her high cheekbones and pockmarked like a lunar surface.

The next day, over lunch, we told Mamma Mercy who we'd met and she filled us in with everything she knew about Billie Holiday.

"That woman ought to be richer than a millionaire," she said, raising the ghost finger she didn't have to lend added weight to her words. She said that the criminals she'd loved had stolen everything, even her name. She told us about how she was raped as a girl by a neighbor, prison, the gossip about her drug addiction, police harassment, and how everyone had an opinion about her sexuality, her past, her talent, and what kinds of punishment would really teach her a lesson. She was black, successful, sang better than all the white singers put together, and the American public loved her. She wouldn't be forgiven a single misstep.

We got into the habit of going to the den where we met her. We always arrived at the same time and sat on the same decrepit sofa to wait for her. She always turned up in a new dress, in different eye shadow than the last time and the black kohl that kept her gaze razor sharp. She ran into our hairy talcum-powdered arms. Ava and I were thrilled; it was a gift to be paid special attention by a woman like her.

"Ava and Maria, you glorious bitches!" she'd say, arms on her hips. "Make some room for this sad old whore."

She collapsed down on the sofa and stayed with us. Flanked by her girls, she ignored everyone else. And every night, like an onion, she'd remove layers and layers of dresses until she had exposed the wounded, bleeding seed, her heart, her secret name.

Immediately after we met, she began to open up as if we were her best friends. She told us that sometimes she couldn't get out of bed, she was so depressed about her breakup with her husband, Louis, who'd used her money to buy mansions in California and convertibles while she had to borrow money from her friends to pay the rent. She wasn't allowed to sing in the bars and clubs in New York where she'd made her name because of a stupid law that prevented anyone who'd been in prison for longer than a year from appearing onstage. She'd been in prison for precisely three hundred and sixty-six days. It seemed impossible that this woman who dressed like a queen lived worse than us, a pair of Latina travestis lost in Harlem.

The more we saw of her, the more otherworldly her friendship seemed. I don't think that Ava or I had ever fallen so deeply in love, not even with a man. And all that, so far, without ever having heard one of her records.

After a while, Ava bought *Lady Sings the Blues* and we finally educated ourselves, listening to it over and over again in disbelief that this was the same woman who shared her marijuana and paid for our beers.

She always wore a gold bracelet with a very elegant diamond that looked lovely on her skinny, dark wrist. The diamond drove me crazy, like a cat chasing a beam of light. She must have gotten tired of me staring at the jewel so much, because she haughtily took it off and put it in my hands.

"Here, so you don't have to go around staring at other people's diamonds like a starving dog."

I couldn't accept it. I was too embarrassed. Billie walked around Harlem and all of goddamned New York as though she weren't famous. When you saw her mink coat or the gleam of her diamonds, you realized that she wasn't the bum you thought she was in those stained tweed pants with holes from ciga-rette ash. She was a star! And she was happy to go out in public with a pair of travestis on her arm! My friends, she'd say, staring defiantly back at passersby.

We saw her so often, sharing joints and tissues, that Ava decided to invite her over for breakfast as we fled from the dawn like vampires. She came and stayed until late, until it was almost night again, thrilled with Mamma Mercy and our tattered wigs and dresses. Tattered but sexy, in our defense. She came over for breakfast many times. After our nightly rounds, we scurried to Mamma Mercy like cats for their bowl of milk, just as the sky was reddening with the dawn. We fell asleep a mess, with our wigs still on and our dicks still suffocating beneath the pant-ies that hid our *chilango* treasures. Mamma Mercy served us coffee, rolls with butter and honey, warm milk, bacon, chicken sandwiches, or huevos rancheros that I'd taught her to make myself. After all the joints we'd smoked, we were ravenous enough to eat Mamma Mercy herself but in the end, after laying waste to the table as if it was the last breakfast we'd ever have, we'd sit back panting with drooping eyelids. Billie slept with us upstairs. We shoved the beds together to make one big enough for the three of us and lay down like newly born pups, having barely pulled down the zips on our dresses, our wigs thrown off haphazardly, like underwear after a night of love. When we woke up, at lunchtime, we were happy to be together, to be part of a friendship that was much better than love.

"Hey, Billie," Ava whispered one morning after we'd woken up all tangled together. "Why do you spend so much time with us?"

"Ever since Louis left, I don't know what to do with my days."

She didn't have many other friends. One of them was a giant guitar player who accompanied her at some of her concerts and had bigger muscles and hairier arms than any man I'd ever seen. We'd dubbed her La Gran Lesbiana but because we couldn't call her that to her face we called her Lagran. Ava and I used to joke about how much we liked the masculine way she played, like she was tickling a girl's thighs. She was a good friend to Billie but she couldn't always be with her. She liked us a lot and always paid for our drinks. Good girls, she'd say, what are you doing tonight, you good Latina girls? We couldn't resist her charms. We suspected she was a lesbian because it was how our minds worked, we were so predictable. But the truth is that she loved Holiday, even when she got bratty from the drink. Everyone ran away, except for Lagran.

I have the feeling that Billie loved her solitude as much as she hated it, because it gave her the energy to sing with her belly full of whiskey, liters and liters of whiskey. She didn't speak to anyone when she was locked away and alone. Maybe she needed to be alone to be at peace. But very often, once she had it, she didn't know what to do with it. You had to experience authentic, complete solitude to be able to do what she did with her voice. Sometimes she'd hum while we were walking through the streets of Harlem and all her talent would show through what was little more than a musical whisper. Walking with a woman like that sent us into a trance. By now we were experts in her back catalogue, with the advice of Mamma Mercy, who lent us records and made newspaper cuttings for us to read. Even though we were so close, we'd never heard her play live. With an orchestra and all that, I mean. We'd never seen her standing in front of a microphone. But there wasn't much work for Billie Holiday and, to tell the truth, she seemed to be taking a break from all the fuss and exposure, not just from the audience, but from the nightly temptations as well.

Sometimes she'd come to the salon and ask us to straighten her hair. We slathered it in goose fat, then we'd attach giant curlers, very tight, and put her under a dryer with a magazine in her hand. We tried to fix her nails but it was no good, she bit them, ate them all away, gnawed on them like a chicken bone. The edges were always bitten raw; she was always bleeding from somewhere on a body that was also growing thinner by the day. We gave her makeovers as if she was the doll we'd never been able to play with as little girls and she let us do it, all meek and submissive. Sometimes we even heard her snoring as we washed her hair.

Her hair was dry and mistreated, but when she let loose the ponytail she always wore, she looked like an Amazon recently arrived in New York. She always liked to have it up and pulled back tight so that it smoothed out the wrinkles around her eyes and fore-head. A couple of her teeth were rotten, but no one had perfect teeth back then. Just white movie and radio stars. Sometimes not even Humphrey Bogart.

One afternoon she came to Mamma Mercy's house in such a good mood that the air around her felt lighter, filled with laughter. The kids in the street playing hide-and-seek had been joking with her while she waited for us to open the door.

"My mom says that you're a singer," said one of the little rascals.

"If you're a singer, sing," challenged another, hiding behind a lamppost.

"I don't have anything to prove to you, devil's children!" she answered, laughing.

"Then give us some money. If you aren't going to sing, give us some change," a little girl piped up.

Billie reached into her handbag as though she was looking for a coin to give the girl but then she hesitated. Instead, she shouted up at our window:

"Open up already, these kids are trying to shake me down. They've even got a front man! Look at this little beauty, the prettiest eyes in America!" she said, pointing at the little scrounger.

Mamma Mercy opened the door.

"You'd better not be bothering the lady!"

They whistled back and went on hustling for coins. Billie looked down at the one who'd asked first, winked, and dropped a coin into a plant pot by the door so the boys couldn't see. We watched Billie's act of generosity from the upstairs window and the good feeling lasted all afternoon. She'd brought vegetables and chicken she'd gotten on the way and a bottle of mint liqueur she was planning to finish over dinner. There was a skip in her step. She was going to appear in a show with a very reputable band, worthy of her, at the Onyx in Harlem. It was a little clandestine, it wouldn't be advertised, but it was going to be a great night. She knew it.

"Come and see me. If I see you in the audience, it'll be easier for me. Don't worry about the money, you'll come as my guests."

And so, Mamma Mercy, Ava, and I went. Beforehand, Billie visited the salon so we could do her hair and makeup and then she went to practice with the pianist who'd be accompanying her, who she said made the piano shriek instead of playing music. We did her hair and then ran off to change for the club. We held our heads high, thrilled and excited about finally being able to see Billie sing. On this occasion we didn't go as travestis; we hid in our men's clothes so we could go to the jazz club without any trouble. Maybe Ava, with her Nordic beauty, might have passed unnoticed. Or maybe not. Best not to find out. Pants, shirt, flat-heeled shoes, and a few drops of perfume behind the ear so as not to lose ourselves in the disguise. Mamma Mercy finally came out of her kitchen. She was wearing a shiny new dress and satin gloves that covered her missing finger. We had a table reserved for us next to none other than Tallulah Bankhead and other New York notables. We were so overwhelmed by everything that was going on that we found ourselves holding our breath, just in case we broke the spell.

A young white piano player set the mood. Suddenly, the lights went down and the black musicians started to get up onstage with their precious packages and instruments as shiny as their shoes and jewelry.

"If there's one thing I like about men of my race, it's the fact they dress like Gypsies. Look at those rings and watches, so shiny!" said Mamma Mercy.

"Calm down," said Ava. "Your dress is burning up."

We laughed quietly, trying not to make a scene in a place as prestigious and historic as the Onyx. At the bar we saw La Gran Lesbiana with her enormous guitar raised over her head. Excuse me, excuse me, excuse me, good girls, she said as she passed us by. She was so big she could easily have gotten work as a longshoreman. Mamma Mercy said:

"If I'd known she was a lesbian, I'd have given her the key to my house long ago."

"She's butcher than a bull," I answered.

The club owner came out from backstage, stood in front of the microphone, and started crowing like a ringmaster. He was a redhead whose clothes were too tight for him. We were terrified that one of his buttons would pop off his belly and hit us right in the eye. He was sweating a lot and his hands were shaking. It seemed a miracle he didn't drop dead right there onstage.

"Ladies and gentlemen, tonight the Onyx has the honor of welcoming the first lady of jazz, the one and only...Lady Day!"

He leapt offstage, and following the applause and an expectant silence she appeared, dressed in pink satin, her hair pulled back taut with a ribbon. When we did her hair that afternoon, she barked at us to pull harder and add wax so her hair would shine and nothing could get mussed out of place. We pulled as if we were putting on a corset. A pair of strass earrings hung from her mousy ears. I'd like to be able to write it properly, to make you feel what I felt, but I'm not smart enough, I'm sorry. I don't have the words to tell you what a sacred experience that night was. The musicians looked at her with respect, as if they were waiting on an angel. I felt like Juan Diegito in the presence of Saint Guadalupe on the day of her ascension.

The first song was about a lover coming home with someone else's lipstick on his shirt. She told him he didn't have anything to explain, to come up and take off the shirt, she was happy her man was home. She swayed in front of the microphone as she sang, like a reed in the wind. We listened to her, enthralled. I had to cover my face to keep from crying. The second song was about winds blowing hard against us. The third was gentle swing; the beat came from the drummer stroking his cymbals, it was fit to lose yourself in. Ava was frozen in place, looking up at this apparition, Billie Holiday standing on her own in a yellowy glow.

"The piano player doesn't know what he's doing," Mamma Mercy whispered, but I ignored her.

The ballads were like riding a bike through an empty city at night. Gentle like that. It was as though the musicians were holding us up with their music and I felt so light, so impossibly light that the idea of flesh made me sick, I felt sick not to be...if you know what I mean...not a musician playing some kind of instrument but *to be* the music, *to be* a song at least, and not a person. I was depressed to have a body, a body that wasn't mine, that I couldn't dress how I liked, perfume how I wanted, or name whatever I chose. There I was in my man's body, dressed like a man, next to Mamma Mercy and Ava, whose blue eyes had filled with tears, and I felt sad. But her voice..."*Heaven, I'm in heaven...*" It was like an opportunity to live on music alone. *"When we're out together, dancing cheek to cheek..."*

It was the most refined, the most exquisite, the most terribly unique thing that could be done on earth. Have you ever heard it? It's music to put on when the sun comes out, when the morning warms up, when food is cooking, when someone dies, when you sleep with someone, when you cry over someone, when you go to bed, when you're celebrating your birthday, when you're celebrating your death, when you're traveling, when you miss your mother, when you're hungry, when you're drinking, and even as you go to sleep, like a lullaby. I knew it with every fiber in the body I hated but loved too, because it was saying to me: "Listen, Maria, you'll never hear music like this again, a true black mass, this moment shall never, ever be repeated."

She sang as though she were on her own, while we downed bourbon after bourbon, which we were going to insist on paying for even though Billie had told us not to even think about it, that it was all on her. Her eyes were closed, her arms pinned to her sides, snip, snap, her fingers clicking to the beat. When she finished a song, she stretched her arms out to either side to form a cross. All she needed now was to start levitating.

She'd cough between one song and another, and laugh too when she'd gotten the wrong tune. She'd start out singing one thing when it was supposed to be another. Then she'd bark at the pianist:

"You son of a bitch, you could have changed the intro!"

Her eyes were bulging, they looked as though they were about to pop out of her head, she was snorting like a bull, but she put her hand on her belly and went on:

"This song is for a pair of ladies here with me tonight, a round of applause for them."

People clapped as though the order had come from Pius XII himself and we almost wet the shawls we imagined around our shoulders, so deeply moved were we that Billie Holiday herself was winking at us from the stage, as if she was saying: "I mean you, you silly travestis."

She'd gotten to her sixth song and everyone started chanting: "'Strange Fruit'! 'Strange Fruit!'" which Ava and I thought an appropriate compliment.

"Okay, this song is very special to me," she said. The trumpet blew so loud that everyone in the front row felt the gust in their hair. Tallulah shouted: "My love! My queen!" so crazily that we were worried she was going to give herself a heart attack.

"That woman's about to have a stroke, my God!" Ava exclaimed.

But Billie sang and it was the first time I'd ever heard the truth about the slaughter of the Black community. Black people hanging from trees like fruit giving off an aroma of charred flesh. A bitter harvest. And we'd thought that the "strange fruit" comments were a compliment. Even though we'd taken an intensive course in Billie Holiday, we were still pretty ignorant.

"I'm strange fruit too," I whispered too softly for anyone to hear.

The three of us hugged and we didn't care anymore if anyone saw us crying. Fags and tears. Billie finished the song in a wail, her eyes glassy and exhausted, as if she didn't have the strength to go on. The club exploded with shouts and applause, except for a couple of bastards sitting at the bar. They were drinking wine and calling out obscenities, insulting the band, trying to provoke the waiters, and harassing any woman who passed by. The people sitting at the tables told them to be quiet but they were looking for a fight.

The next song was "All I Have Is Yours," and before it got to the chorus, the rude pair at the bar got up and shouted:

"New York Police!" with such authority that Billie stopped singing and slipped offstage in the blink of an eye. "You don't have a license for this show," howled the older cop.

The club owner went over to talk to them and Mamma Mercy ran through her rosary of curses: bastards, sons of bitches, motherfucking sons of whores. I got ready to break a bottle on the table to defend Billie if they tried to arrest her, and I knew that Ava would back me up.

But it didn't go that far. Billie Holiday was smuggled into a car that then screeched off down the streets of Harlem and ended up at Mamma Mercy's place. They had to break in and we found her sitting at the table when we got there.

"I'm sorry about the door, we'll get it fixed tomorrow."

She was depressed at not being able to finish the concert.

We made coffee in a blackened pot and she told us she needed a place to hide out. Things like that always happened, the police were obsessed with her, they even followed her into the bathroom. They wanted to prove that they were doing something about drugs and Billie was a useful example. It was like they were saying: "Look, we've arrested Billie

Holiday, see? It doesn't matter who you are." Billie swore blind, crossing her chest, that she was clean. That she only drank alcohol. That the heroin days were long gone.

Mamma Mercy had made her up a bed with clean sheets and drawn a warm bath before she'd finished her account of her sorrows. The evening of the next day, Ava and I went to her apartment to fetch her dresses, makeup, two most expensive furs, and a roll of dollar bills hidden behind the toilet that we didn't dare count but looked like a lot.

Ava and I split our shifts at the hairdresser's. She worked in the morning and I in the afternoon so there was always someone at home to stay with her when Mamma Mercy went out shopping or to visit one of her lovers.

"My bodyguards are a pair of fairies!" she'd say, laughing. "If Louis ever showed up here, he'd beat the shit out of all of us."

She said that Louis was a man who packed a punch. She'd seen him beat up professional boxers and dangerous goons. Her man could knock down a cement wall.

"I'll be ready with my rolling pin," said Ava, brandishing Mamma Mercy's huge pin. It had already cracked a few skulls in its time.

"But, honey, you can't even lift it. You're such a fairy even a woman's stronger than you!" she laughed back.

She got up very early in the morning and turned on the radio to listen to opera until well into the afternoon. She made coffee and helped us with our bags for the salon, and barely ever went out onto the street.

No ex-husband came looking for her. No dealer came to bang down our door. Not even Lagran, her guitar player, turned up. The only person who noticed that something was up was Mandy, who lived on the corner. She asked about the mysterious goings-on at home, why she never saw us in the neighborhood, why we didn't go to the smoking dens anymore, and what was wrong with Mamma Mercy, who only ever showed her face once a week to buy the groceries.

Because I knew that stuff like this ate away at her, I flapped my scarf coquettishly:

"We're hiding a jazz star from journalists."

"I don't believe you," Mandy answered.

"Come and see for yourself. Say you're making donuts and you ran out of oil."

That afternoon she turned up and Billie opened the door, but because she was pig ignorant Mandy didn't know who she was.

"You lied, she's not famous, she's just an ordinary black woman," Mandy chided me the next day as I was on my way to relieve Ava at the salon.

We lost count of how many days, or weeks, Billie spent as the guest of honor in our home. It was as though we'd always lived together. But one afternoon, when I'd taken over from Ava, who'd gone searching for treasure in the pants of black men, Mamma Mercy stormed into the salon. The customers shrieked in fright at the sight of her; her huge ox thighs, her eyes bursting out of her head, and her heart in her mouth.

"Girl! What's got into you? You look like you've seen a ghost!"

"It's Bi…Bi…Billie. She's bad."

"What do you mean, bad?" I asked.

"She started gnawing on the table and groaning like an animal."

I left my customer's half-done hair to my assistant and ran home with Mamma Mercy. We ran so fast we almost gave ourselves a heart attack.

We burst into the house, the faggot overwhelmed by the drama and the busty matron always ready to help. We called out to Billie, quietly at first and then loud, but the damn woman wasn't anywhere to be seen. I was terrified we'd find her dead or, I don't know, that Louis had dragged her off.

We went up to the bathroom and I found her there, up to her neck in water. The water was boiling and the steam in the room was suffocating. Billie hadn't gotten undressed; she was wearing her white sweater and there was her poor hair, all crisped from being straightened so often with tongs. The steam from the bath burned our faces.

Mamma Mercy was stunned by the sight of the lady scalding herself in the bath.

"Don't be afraid," Billie said.

"The water's very hot, honey," I answered.

"Don't worry. I'm fine, I can stand it."

"Are you trembling?"

"I got the urge for a little horse."

We helped her out together and it was as though she was being born for a second time, soaking wet, with her spindly legs and wrinkled knees like an ancient face, those paper arms and the shaking that came from deep inside. We dried her off, covered her with a newly pressed robe, and sat her down by the woodstove, on which we put a lovely chicken stew to heat up.

After dinner, Mamma Mercy sat her huge ass down on the worn leather sofa she'd inherited from a white former employer to drink a brandy and smoke her moldy black tobacco. She laughed long and hard thinking about the salon customers' faces when she had come in. Then came Ava, tired out from her treasure hunting. We slowly combed our wigs, like we did every night. Holiday, exhausted, lay down on her host's lap. Our friendship played out in silence, each with their own music. I have no idea what Mamma Mercy's, Billie's, or Ava's music was, but I can tell you about mine; it was the dream of a house in Florida, close to the rivers and the sea, with flowers in my hair, loving one man, and another and another, and never suffering over any of them.

A whole lifetime must have passed before Mamma Mercy sent us all to bed. Billie shuddered, a little annoyed.

"Fucking hell." She'd wet herself, the robe, and the sofa.

One day we all went out together dressed in the best that Billie's wardrobe had to offer. We were decked out in so many jewels, beads, sequins, stones, and crystals that we felt like walking Times Squares. We went for a beer in a bar frequented by brilliant young jazz players. Billie was hoping to cross paths with Lester Young, her President. Lester had very sad eyes and played the most elegant blues you can imagine on his saxophone. He was a shy, sensitive guy, the kind God doesn't make anymore. I like guys who know how to be afraid.

"That's Pres," Billie told us. "I miss him. I'm in this shit without him, without my mother, without my husband..."

In one of the newspaper clippings that Mamma Mercy kept for us, there was a story with the headline "The End of a Friendship?," which had a photograph of Lester Young and Billie in a recording studio. It was recent; she looked a lot like the Billie we knew. In the photograph he's laughing, as though at a joke, and she's making some kind of statement, passionately, maybe scolding him, with a cigarette between her fingers. The story reported two rumors about them. One said that Lester was in love with Billie's mother and was upset about their arguments and the scenes Lady Day made when she was angry with her mother. It even said that they'd come to blows more than once, slapping each other in public.

We didn't really believe it but neither did we care how our friend got along with her mother. But according to the gossip rags it was one of the reasons that the honeyed saxophonist who was Lester Young had distanced himself from Holiday.

The article moved on to the second rumor, which was much crueler: that Lester was head-over-heels in love with Billie and she didn't see him as a suitable match. She'd laughed in his face when she rejected him, she'd have to be crazy to kiss him, she saw him only as a "musical lover" and that would have to be enough. The fact was that they weren't speaking, but in the cutting Mamma Mercy had kept for us, nobody cared about that.

Whatever their history, when Billie spoke about him that night, her eyes beat like a heart. So the three of us went. Ava and I were scared to death because a black cat had crossed our paths the moment we stepped out of the house and that was a very bad sign. But we went to a bar full of famous figures from the black community and what do you know? A little blond man, whiter than chalk, with a jawline like a mechanical digger, raised his glass to me from afar.

"It's Gerry!" Billie crowed, bothering the whole bar. "Come sit with us, you son of a bitch!"

Gerry came to sit at our table and looked us in the eye, each of us, at length before addressing Billie:

"Louis's looking for you. He says you owe him a mink coat."

"He gave it to me with my money, I don't owe him a thing. I sold it. I needed money to eat."

"He said he was going to mash up your kidneys if you didn't come with either the coat or the money from the damned coat."

"I sold it to this beautiful young lady here with me today," she said, squeezing Ava's knee. Ava got the message.

"You need to take better care of yourself. Webster and I want to get together and do something. And we'd like you to join us."

That night Lester didn't turn up and Billie grew despondent. It happened to her regularly. She'd be the happiest woman in the world and then suddenly the saddest. She could cross the road with a kid who'd smiled at her, pick him up, buy him candy and shower him in kisses, laughing all the while. She was so good that one day she might say: "Enough of this," and start cleaning the house from top to bottom and end to end, making everything sparkle, and at light speed too. And just as easily she could collapse onto a sofa and down bottle after bottle of gin until she passed out.

The night she didn't find Lester she was bitter.

That week she told us that she was moving back to her apartment; if Louis hadn't found her by now, it meant he wasn't coming.

"I'll bet he's trying to get dollars out of Ella Fitzgerald's fat ass. He'll leave me alone, I'm sure of it," she said.

But before leaving, she sent us on a delivery to Sarah Vaughan at the theater she played, leaving her a mysterious small box wrapped carefully in blue French velvet. We went together and were able to deliver it into the hands of Vaughan herself, who behaved, it has to be said, like a kindly, smiling angel.

"A gift from Lady Day, Miss Vaughan."

"Oh, what can it be? From her...that girl, that girl, that girl," she said, still smiling.

She saw us off with nothing but love and kisses, saying she always needed help with her hair, she'd call us to come do it ourselves, she'd always envied Billie's impeccable hair: "A true star," she said.

Billie told us that she'd sent her Sarah's husband's underwear, which he'd left in her bed a few months before, with a note that read: "A piano between us and any song you like until one of us is worn out."

Billie collapsed into fits of laughter thinking of poor Sarah Vaughan's face when she saw the gift she'd sent, and even though she'd treated us so well, we had to agree she deserved it after Billie let us in on a few things. She said that when she was released from prison, she'd felt lost and alone in New York and went looking for familiar faces and old friends. So she went to see Sarah at her theater, the way any of us might, seeking out a friend after going through a bad time.

"When she sang in dive bars dressed in rags, I sent her a couple of my best dresses so that when people saw her dressed as a star, they'd treat her like one."

She'd protected Vaughan from the police when they started sniffing around for drugs under the misapprehension that that was what friends did. But instead of being a friend, the night that she went to see Vaughan at the theater after leaving prison, Vaughan refused to see her. Years later, the bitch explained herself saying that her husband had told her not to. It wasn't good for her career to be seen with an ex-convict.

"I don't know why we get punished for taking revenge. No one appreciates suffering," Billie finished with a laugh.

When she left, the house felt empty, as if it had been stripped from the inside. She went back to her apartment with only her tenacity to protect her. She left alone, with her bags and a basket of rolls we'd baked for her along with ham, cheese, and fruit, getting into a taxi that took her down the street, far from our friendship.

It was at least four months before we saw her again. We'd started to suspect that something was wrong when we realized she wasn't performing anywhere. We looked for her in all the bars and smoking dens we could with our hearts in our mouths, but with no luck.

We went to her apartment but there was no answer. We started a vigil, day and night, outside her door but there was no sign of her. Ava started at midday and I relieved her in the afternoon; we walked around the block, coming and going but bearing in mind that nobody likes to see a faggot wandering around their neighborhood. There was no answer when we rang her doorbell and every day that passed without our seeing her, the knot in our stomachs grew a little tighter. Then one night she finally came back to the smoking den where we'd met her. She was scrawny, like algae stuck to a stone on a riverbed, her complexion was raw, her cheeks were hollow, just empty spaces beneath her eyes, and her teeth were even more rotten. Her shoulders were bare and bony, the kind you see on a gargoyle.

"What do you want? I drink gin for breakfast and dinner."

Once again, she rolled one of her mind-blowing joints and stepped away from the crowd of admirers that followed her everywhere. She wasn't entirely comfortable. The place had changed a lot in a few months and we didn't recognize the clientele anymore. Black or white, it didn't look like anyone had treasure in their pants. They seemed more likely to be full of bugs and spiny reptiles. She asked us to walk her home.

"I've got a few things I want to give you," she said.

We went there, an ordinary apartment, distressingly bare. Just a pine table and three rickety chairs that looked as if they were going to give up the ghost at any moment, a record player, a couple of records in the corner, and a photo of her and her Chihuahua. In her fridge a bottle of milk had begun the slow transformation into bitter cheese and the bed was covered with a pair of coats instead of a duvet. Her dresses, shoes, and the little jewelry she had left were strewn across the apartment like traffic signs, like little reminders, a way not to get lost in the poverty that was once sheer luxury.

"Bad loves," she murmured.

She put on one of her records from a few years ago when her voice was much younger and clearer than it was now, and then she started making a chicken stew.

"Let's have some breakfast, ladies."

She told us that the producer of her new record had paid a bribe to let her sing in a bar, I can't remember the name right now.

"I never thought I'd sing again, but when you start thinking like that, you die."

She had to promote her songs but it was very hard for her to stay sober, especially when she was always having to find musicians to accompany her at the last minute, novices who asked her what key to play in, who couldn't follow her down her labyrinthine musical paths.

While the stock and chicken worked their magic, she went to her room and brought back several dresses, which were now too big for her.

"I don't think I'll be getting any fatter."

We ate her stew and then, like we were sisters, she led us into the bedroom and took a crumpled piece of paper out from beneath her bed. It was a single bed and the sheets were covered in cigarette burns. She straightened it out and showed it to us: "You're going to pay for every lost cent in blood."

"Louis came to visit a few days ago. He tried to kick the door down, but the damn thing wouldn't give. Then he wrote this."

"Why don't you sell your furs and give him the money?"

"Because I wanted to leave them to you," she said, shrugging.

We wouldn't have accepted them. We went on trying to persuade her to sell the mink at least, which was apparently worth eighteen thousand dollars, but she'd have rather seen it burn than give the money to her ex-husband. No, sir.

After that night, it wasn't so difficult for us to find her anymore, and she came a few times to visit us at Mamma Mercy's house because she missed our chilaquiles in the morning and our pozole at lunch. And she was right to come, it was the only time she ever ate properly. But even though she was just skin and bones she still rescued us from the most humiliating night of our lives. The police picked us up in a smoking den and made us stand nude in the station parking lot, tied to a mast like indigenous martyrs, them throwing buckets of freezing water over us again and again, shouting the worst things you can imagine. And just when we didn't have a shred of dignity left, we heard an uproar in one of the offices that sounded like the end of the world and we knew that she'd come to help us. She'd heard about our arrest from street sweepers the very same night.

She demanded our immediate release, offering to buy dinner for the whole station if they got us back on our feet quickly. She'd brought men's clothes we assumed belonged to Louis.

"These sons of bitches are wearing my dresses, they're coming with me," she declared to everyone in earshot in a tone that brooked no contradiction.

We went back to her apartment that night, sleeping on the floor under a pile of dresses, letters from her admirers, and coats.

One afternoon Ava was at home nursing Mamma Mercy, who had contracted an embarrassing venereal disease from her lover, Don Leonardo Muñiz, a Colombian determined to take Harlem by storm with his high-voltage accordion. We called him the black swallow because he came and went from town to town with the change of the seasons. He must have taken a wrong turn during his eternal wandering and Mamma Mercy was paying for it. The penicillin sent her straight to bed, almost delirious, so one of us had to take care of her and clean the house.

I was at the hairdresser's, trying to add volume to the sparse hair of a customer who left good tips. They were well deserved, of course, because you needed to work magic to make her hair look good. As I was brushing and spraying, I started to feel sad. I don't know how, but it happened just like that, from one second to the next. With the old lady's skull in my hands, a bad feeling came over me. I'm an intuitive travesti. It's as though the air were whispering to me, telling me things. I went on in spite of the shiver that ran down my spine; there was no getting away from my octogenarian hairdo.

I don't know whether I ever told you the name they knew me by at the salon. But I'll repeat it just in case: Carlos. My male name is Carlos Montoya. Fortunately, my customers called me Charlie and I liked how it sounded: *Chooorly*.

Forgive me, I'm getting distracted. There I was, listening to my customer complaining that her children only visited her when they needed money, when La Gran Lesbiana came in with a crazy expression on her face, just like Mamma Mercy when Billie got into the bath full of scalding water. She was terrified, the poor thing.

"I'm looking for Maria," she called from the door, and everyone turned to look at her.

"Maria's a friend of mine. Who's asking for her?" I interrupted, and she finally recognized me.

She came over and whispered into my ear. My hands were holding a round brush and a can of hairspray and I crossed them in a kind of beautician's talisman to ward off whatever she had to tell me:

"Billie needs you. She's asking for you."

I said that a friend of mine was in trouble and without waiting for anyone to give me permission or worrying who'd finish off the old woman's hair, I ran off to Billie's house faster than I'd ever run before. Faster than I'd ever run for anyone. I left La Gran Lesbiana behind at the salon, scared to death.

I don't think my feet touched the ground before I got to Billie's apartment. I came to a sudden halt at her door and knocked.

"Maria?" she asked.

"Yes, honey."

She came to open the door.

"Come on in, you old bitch."

As she let me in, she was holding a steak over her eye. Her pajamas were covered in blood. The apartment was a mess, as if a tornado had ripped through it. It had been emptied of its record player, radio, records, furs, and knickknacks. There was, however, a glass of mint liqueur on the table. And a syringe and a plate. She was wearing an old pink matelassé robe with nothing underneath. There was an unpleasant stench of iodine, like in a hospital room. Or a mortuary.

"It was terrible, Maria. He bounced me off the walls like a rubber ball."

"No one came to help?"

"I tried to cry out, but he covered my mouth and hit me in the stomach."

Oh, Billie, my love. You should have stayed with us. We'd have gotten your career back on track, we'd have sworn to anything in front of the judges, we'd have cried, we'd have organized petitions, we'd have burned down the whole fucking world just to stop you from having to go through any of this. Away from us, you were in danger, that's a fact.

I took her into the bedroom. Her whole body smelled of mint liqueur. I laid her down, leaving the steak on her eye.

"To keep the swelling down," she murmured.

"Everything's going to be fine. Don't try to speak. I need to call a doctor to check you for broken bones."

"I'd know. Don't call anyone..." She stopped to take a breath. The bruises were beginning to appear, green and purple blotches on her arms and legs. "Stay with me, don't call anyone."

I sat down on the floor next to the bed and listened to her rocky breathing. Fear gave way to calm and I started to breathe more easily too. I thought about how I needed to go home to let them know what had happened, relieve Ava, get her to come over here. And cook for Mamma Mercy, who was also in pain.

I fantasized about tracking down Billie's ex-husband, dressed in black, waiting for him for as long as it would take, unseen in the darkness. I'd pounce before he had time to blink. Kick his ass for what he did.

Suddenly, Billie began to sob, solemnly, as if a story was coming to an end.

"He took the mink I wanted to give you," she wailed, taking the steak from her eye.

She looked terrible. The eye wouldn't open, it was bruised and her eyelid was swollen up like a plump plum. She had dried blood on her forehead and temple.

"Shhhh...my darling...shhh..."

"Maria..."

"What?"

"You're like a caress, you know? You're wonderful...wonderful."

"Shhh..."

"You're nice, you make women pretty and when you wear bright dresses you look like Frances Farmer, in that blond wig that suits you so well."

She coughed, followed by a groan so heartrending that the whole apartment shook.

"Don't try to speak, you'll feel better when you get some sleep."

"That night at the Onyx...I was looking down at you from the stage and saw your eyes fill with tears..."

"Yes, Billie, it was wonderful, but try to sleep so I can go make a phone call."

"Don't leave me alone."

"I need to let the people at the salon know I'm fine and get someone to tell Ava to come join us."

"But I want to be with you."

"Shhh…"

"I want you to hug me."

Then I felt her bony hand on my cheek, a cheek-bone I prayed wasn't rough with a beard, and on my neck. She pinched my nipple.

"It was horrible, Maria. He hit me, he spit in my mouth, he pissed on my clothes."

"Okay, okay, it's over now, the moment you're back on your feet you're going to come live with us."

Then there was a silence as she held her breath.

"I want you to make love to me."

"Beloved Virgin of Guadalupe, the things you say."

"I mean it. I need you to make love to me, to embrace me, to be naked beside me."

"Stop it, it's not funny. Stop fucking around."

But her hands were still all over me, tangled in my hair, my short male hair. She sat up on the pillow with a moan, but this time there was lust mixed in with the pain and she kissed me on the mouth. I caught the scent of her blood and felt nauseated.

"I mean it."

"But I'm no man, how can I?"

"I don't need a man. I need my friend Maria… I want Maria to cuddle me."

She took off my shirt, button by button, her decrepit lungs purring at me close to my mouth, then she shoved her hand down my pants and I started to cry. She told me not to worry, we weren't doing anything wrong. And before I knew it, I was naked beside her, with my unshaven, rough nipples and her cadaverous little body covered in bruises her bastard ex-husband had left as a souvenir.

She continued whispering to me, close to my mouth, words I didn't understand but that bamboozled me with their smell, and suddenly I was inside her, penetrating her, thrusting carefully to keep from hurting her, and she kept still, with the eye that still opened wide, staring inside me, knowing all of me. Everything in the room smelled bad, even my shame had its own distinctive stink, something unforgettable, like the night she rescued us from the police station. I didn't understand what was happening to my body, why my penis was rebelling, willing to get hard just then, with her. I wasn't feeling any sensations I could identify, I didn't recognize anything going on down there or inside me. But I kept moving very gently while she moaned.

"I'm going to come," I warned.

It was quick, like a slap.

I came and began to cry, I didn't know why. She was exhausted and went straight to sleep. I got dressed and walked out on tiptoe. I went home.

———

I cried again as I told my fellow concubines the state in which I found Billie, but I didn't mention the clumsy way I had offered consolation. Ava went to take care of her that night and was then relieved by La Gran Lesbiana. I think Carmen McRae, one of the few friends Billie had left, helped too. So the swelling around the eye went down and the bruises faded.

I didn't visit her again. Ava kept me informed. Sometimes I sent her with letters Billie never answered. I knew she was hurt by my disappearing act but I had no choice. I couldn't get over what we'd done together. What she'd made me do. It shattered all my cozy assumptions about love. She'd danced in front of me and I'd penetrated her, a woman! It made me feel that all my time as a fag had been worth nothing. Going through all that suffering to become a woman and ending up in bed with one. And making love to her on top of that.

I could be happily working at the salon, or at home, and suddenly the sight of her body would come to me, her vagina like a dark fig split in half. Full of seeds. It was like making love to an enormous fig, gasping and moaning. I needed to get rid of those thoughts, they were driving me crazy. The shame.

Ava came and went, taking care of her for the both of us, covering for me. And on her trips between the two apartments, as though the fact she was taking care of someone gave her the confidence to embrace her destiny, she decided to put her men's clothes in a drawer and stick definitively to dresses, which she'd never take off again.

Sometimes I wanted to ask whether Billie had propositioned her too. But I didn't dare. If she did, Ava didn't think it reason enough to abandon her.

Mamma Mercy visited her regularly too. Sometimes they went together. They went with her to one of her last television appearances, for which they did her hair and makeup. They cooked and left her enough food for two or three days, forcing her to eat. Neither of them asked why I didn't go with them. I guess she must have filled them in.

They brought me her last record, *Lady in Satin*, in which she's accompanied only by strings. It's my favorite record, I'll always say so. She'd written a dedication: "Maria, I'm a fool to want you. Billie." It was accompanied by a kiss in earth-colored lipstick.

Some time later, we heard on the grapevine that she'd been admitted to the Metropolitan Hospital in police custody. They'd found heroin under her pillow.

We went to the hospital every day but were never allowed to see her.

She passed away without a sound, still in the hospital, like she-wolves when they get old and look for a place to die. On her body, they found a roll of bills, about twenty dollars, tucked into her sock.

I'm writing this from prison, where I've been for the past six years for defending Ava from a son of a bitch who was about to beat her to death. It was a spectacular way to end the chapter. The police found me lying on top of the thug's body with my Frances Farmer wig in one hand and a stone ashtray in the other.

I'd have done that for Billie, Mamma Mercy, or Ava. I'd do it again. This man's strength has to be good for something.

I turned myself in, coming along without complaint. I knew that it would give me a chance to rest a little. I'd have lovers, the boys would like me, I'd form covens with the fags, and I'd be the queen of manual labor. Inside, no one would judge me if I confessed that not only did I make love to Billie Holiday, but I also stole her gold and diamond bracelet. She'd left it right there, on top of one of the few tables left in the house, as if she didn't care.

I would have returned it if she missed it. But she never even noticed it was gone.

AFTERNOON TEA

"Grandma...why are we brown?"

The grandmother puts down the rifle she's been cleaning. Another rifle and a box of ammunition are sitting on the kitchen table in front of her.

"What?"

"Why are we brown?"

"We're not brown, we're *morochas*. Where did you hear that?"

"We were in gym class and Tati shouted, 'Ewww!!! She has brown nipples!'"

The kettle comes to a boil and the grandmother stands up to turn off the burner. She wraps a dish-cloth around the iron handle before picking up the kettle. Then she puts two bags of coffee in one mug and a tea bag in the other and pours in the hot water before bringing both mugs to the table. The sugar and spoons are already laid out on the cloth. She unwraps the bread, which has been bundled up in cloth to keep warm. It came out of the clay oven less than an hour ago.

"How did she see your nipples?" she asks, sitting down.

"We were finishing gym class and had to get changed back into dry clothes. So I was sweaty and took off my T-shirt and she saw my boobies. Why are we brown?"

"We're not brown." The grandmother sips from her mug, which she holds in two hands. Her gold wedding ring is shoved right up to the top of her finger, where it meets the palm. "'Brown' is the wrong word, it's a filthy color. We're *morochas*, which is different." She sips from her mug but the coffee is burning hot and scalds her throat. The grandmother grimaces in pain and tears come into her eyes. Her granddaughter laughs. "We're not brown, we're *morochas*, okay?"

"But that's not an answer." The girl puts two heaped spoonfuls of sugar into her tea, adds milk, cuts two slices of bread, and dips them in too. The bread swells with milky tea and she starts to scoop it up with the spoon like soup.

"We're *morochas* because the paint ran out while we were being made."

"What paint?"

"At the place where people are made they didn't have enough paint to make us really dark. We were going to be black, but they ran out of paint in the color department. There are a lot of people like us in the world. We didn't get so many coats. But they didn't paint white people at all, or only gave them very thin coats, which is why they get hurt so easily. Sometimes you just have to poke them for them to turn red as a tomato."

"You're making things up."

"No, I'm not. It's not me who says so, the old women do."

"You're old."

"Yes, but there are plenty older, believe me."

"So why did Tati say 'Ewww' when she saw my brown nipples?"

"Because she's an idiot. Only idiots say things like that. It's better to be *morocha*. She can be as gringa as she likes but at the place where people are made they didn't bother to paint her. They must have had a good reason." She sips her coffee again, more carefully this time, before continuing. "And there are a lot of advantages to being *morocha*. Colors look better on you: red, orange, yellow. Put a yellow dress on that girl who said ewww about your nipples and see how it looks on her. Personally, I'd much rather look good in yellow. And as if that weren't enough, you can go out when it's sunny without turning red like an iguana or burning your skin as easily as this Tati girl. And there's something else: *morochas* age better too. Look at your grandmother's skin."

The grandmother presents her face to her grand-daughter framed in her hands as though it were a jewel, something to be treasured. First one cheek, then the other, then the cheekbones. "Look, look at your grandmother's skin." She lifts her chin with her eyes closed, showing off her neck. Then she undoes her yellow dress to show the girl her collarbones, look at your grandmother's skin, good and dark, the bones in my chest, look, look. The old woman holds up her forearm in profile; it gleams in the sun like a sword.

"Look. Not bad for seventy-three. Just fresh cream and the sun. If it weren't for the sand and dust you get in August and the lime from the quarry, I wouldn't even need the cream. But the dust dries everything out."

The girl still looks terrified: a moment ago she thought that her grandmother was going to undo her shirt all the way to reveal her nipples. Why was she showing off her wrinkles? She decides not to ask, just in case, and continues to sip her spoonfuls of tea-soaked bread. When the bread is gone, she cuts more and dunks it until it falls to pieces. Having finished cleaning the rifles, stimulated by the coffee, the grandmother grows talkative:

"Also, we're worth more..."

"How are we worth more?"

"Darker things are more expensive because they're rarer."

The girl frowns. Why is her grandmother talking like this? The house has sucked up as much light through the windows as it can and now they have to light an oil lamp and candles to see by.

"Think about ebony furniture, it's the darkest wood in the world. Do you know anyone who has an ebony chair?"

"No."

"Of course you don't, because they're so expensive. Do you know anyone who wears a black pearl necklace?"

"No," the girl says, sighing, annoyed by her grandmother's questions. This way she has of asking questions instead of answering hers. Wouldn't it just be easier to say why they're brown?

"You don't know anyone with a black pearl necklace because they cost an arm and a leg and they're very hard to find. And it's not just about money.

Black things are much nicer than any other color. Do you remember the black singer we saw on TV, when you said what a good singer she was and got goose bumps?"

"Yes!" the girl replies, happy at finally being able to say yes to something. There was a time when they had electricity at home and watched television. Life was very different back then.

"Look at black panthers. Black olives! Don't you think blackbirds are prettier than canaries? It's better to be dark."

"What color was Mommy?"

"She was like us. Her friends at school called her tar candy. Tar candy! Tar candy! And she came home crying and said it was my fault. It took a lot of effort to make her understand that it was better to be *morocha*. We could fall asleep in the sun without blistering all over!" She gestures in exasperation, sensing that her words aren't getting through.

"I'd like to be like my friends at school. Like Tati. That color."

The grandmother finishes the last of her coffee and bangs the mug down hard on the table. Her granddaughter jumps in her chair.

"It's getting dark, let's go." The girl puts down a mug whose bottom is sticky with crumbs and follows her grandmother as she picks up the two rifles. They cross the yard, where night is falling fast, leaving footprints in their wake, like the tracks of small vehicles. Bags and bags of earth are piled along the fence. A trench of potato sacks filled with earth. The dusty earth of the region. The grandmother lays down a tarp and kneels on the ground. The girl imitates her. She gives the girl a rifle and she takes it with big, scared eyes, struggling because it's too big and heavy for a girl her age. The grandmother watches her as she sets herself like a soldier. That's right. They lean on the bags of earth and take aim. The house is left empty and all the animals in the yard are asleep. Except for the dogs. The dogs don't sleep while one of them is still awake.

The girl and her grandmother have the eyesight of lynxes. They're as comfortable as ghosts in the dead of night.

"When they come, if any of those bastards gets out of the truck, aim at their head. Don't hesitate," says the grandmother, and her granddaughter adjusts her shoulder, finger on the trigger. She digs her feet into the dust and takes a deep breath. Just as she's been taught.

THE BEARD

Some girlfriends just get lucky. You pass them in the street and they're like, What are you looking at? when the guy walking next to them is hot enough to make a traffic light blush. You just want to go up to them and say, You're a fortunate woman, honey. Then you get the ones with no luck at all, who fall in love with men who treat them badly and they just put up with it in silence. Out of love. Or convenience. Some girlfriends want to be loved more than they are. Then there are the girlfriends who can't find a balance. Girlfriends who can't stop fucking other men. Sleepwalker girlfriends, girlfriends who never wanted to be girlfriends, girlfriends who smash crockery, girlfriends who say yes to everything, girlfriends who forget about their friends. And there's one kind of very rare girlfriend, as rare as an albino crocodile, the girlfriend for hire. Not much is known about them, but there's plenty of conjecture.

The first time was pure chance (I'm revealing all this now because finally, after many years, my first ever client has found his way out of the closet). My friend Marcio Cafferata had to go to his brother's wedding and his parents had begun to nag him about his bachelorhood, because he'd never brought a girl-friend home. Thirty years ago, that was a clue that you might have a gay son. Parents wouldn't stand for faggot offspring. Better dead than a fag. Marcio found the pestering suffocating: his mother's health, the family name, his grandfather's clinics, and their reputation among the declining elite of Córdoba were all apparently at stake.

He was a teenager when his father found a photo of Antonio Banderas in the nude in his history folder. He threw him out of the house. He stayed over at a friend's for several months until his mother tracked him down and begged him to come home before people started to talk. She sent him to a psychologist for conversion therapy. I was the friend who most urged him to come out of the closet, telling him that it was all damp in there, it was better in the light. But we were a different generation; the world was still beautiful and very hostile. The point is that Marcio had to go to a wedding and his father had given him an ultimatum: either he went accompanied by a girl or he'd better start thinking about a different surname.

The wedding day was fast approaching, he'd tried on his tux...and he'd made vain attempts to seduce women at the office and in bars. I mean, the things that family occasions make us do. The night that he suggested it we were standing in line at the La Cochera theater, I can't remember what play we were going to see, I think it was *Divine Kisses*, one where at the end they have a load of brides dressed in white peeing for real onstage. Marcio was deathly pale and it was obvious that he'd ruined his manicure from the nerves. I didn't like to see him in that state, but I couldn't think how to help him.

He just blurted it out:

"Do you want to be my girlfriend for the night of my brother's wedding?"

"Not if I was tortured by Countess Bathory herself. And your parents have met me."

"Just a couple of times. And they were drunk. They don't remember you."

"Of course they do, don't be an idiot..."

"Come on, please. I need a girlfriend. I'll pay you!"

There was a silence and I thought about how my mother always said that all I was good for was ruining the sheets and reflected, why not? Why not just go out one night with my rich friend and show my ma that I'm good at lying too?

"You'll have to dress nicely. Nothing crazy."

"I don't have anything nice."

"Tomorrow, we'll go to the mall so you can get yourself something decent."

The color flooded back into his cheeks and a smile lit up his face. *So that's what gratitude looks like*, I thought. It was as though I'd saved his life. On our way into the theater, we agreed on a few details so we wouldn't contradict each other at the wedding. He asked me just to tell the truth about me and him so we wouldn't have to make anything up except for how we'd started going out and for how long. By the time the play began, we were ready to fool his family.

I don't think I ever went to a more entertaining party, packed full of lovely guys with asses like melons and rhinoceros necks. I worked my charms on them all. I flirted with everyone, even some of the women, the father of the groom and the groom himself. My faux father-in-law never took his eyes off my tits; it was like I kept the Aleph in my cleavage.

"You're lovely!" he cried, pulling me against his hard, ex–rugby player's stomach.

"Don't be such a slut, and stop messing with my dad, I'm begging you," Marcio whispered into my ear.

Halfway through the party, we each took half a tab of acid and danced for two hours in such bliss that it felt as if we were dancing with the galaxy itself. Pretending that I was his girlfriend was the easiest thing in the world. Just think: I set my hair, put on makeup, wore a pretty dress... and Marcio's eyes were as blue as the bottom of a swimming pool, he had a hairy, muscular chest, an ass that restored your faith in God, and a swagger, a way about him that loosened boxers and panties alike.

It went so well that night, his family loved me, that he decided to keep the arrangement going awhile. He needed to deal with the rumors at work too, and among friends of the family.

"Money's not a problem."

I charged him in dollars for every date. Remember that in the nineties the dollar and the peso were of equal value, my darlings. I charged double for family meals. I had enough on my plate with my family so I always charged more for dates that involved relatives. Usually, we planned to go places where we thought people who knew Marcio might be, so we could play out the charade: "Oh, let me introduce you to my girlfriend," or "This is the girl I'm dating." Gradually, word began to spread that

Marcio, with all his gentle ways and mannerisms, was going out with a real, flesh-and-blood woman. And although there are always a few doubters, rumors about his heterosexuality began to stick among his friends, family, and colleagues. They soon forgot their concerns about his manhood. I think that much of his success had to do with the fact that I was a delightful rent-a-girl.

And so that's how my little hustle began, thanks to my friend being in a tight spot. A girl for gays who needed a girlfriend, because it was a matter of life or death at work, or to reassure the parents, or whatever. I'm talking about offering an excellent service as a girlfriend for fags who, for various reasons, had to pretend to be manlier than they were. I've never heard of any other girls doing that. I'd like to think that I was a pioneer, and an exclusive one to boot. I never slept with any of them, much as I might have liked to. With some of them, I could feel the testosterone sloshing around inside, begging for penetration and orgasms. But I was always reserved, polite, and in control. It was useless anyway! I could be as horny as I liked, and I certainly made the most of the kisses we were obliged to share in public, but they wouldn't have touched me with a barge pole. Which is why I charged in dollars. And I was expensive. It was a five-star service.

While I was doing that gig, I gave up my degree in literature, but more because of my relationship with the—married—professor of Latin American Literature II. The affair put an end to my taste for studying and his marriage, on the day of their fourth wedding anniversary. His wife slit her wrists when she found out about it, which I thought was a little much; the professor wasn't worth messing the house up with all that blood. I had to drop out, but thanks to some contacts of my father's I was able to get a job writing a column for *El Centro* newspaper. And because that didn't take up much of my time, my father also hired me as his secretary. That's me, the rainbow sheep of the family. My mother is an architect, my father a doctor specializing in infectious diseases. My mother always said she wanted to travel the world, and never get tied down to anything, but she ended up married to the most sedentary person alive. I was always the ugliest of the Montegrosos' three children. Our relatives and parents' friends gave me hurtful nicknames: the monkey, the bat, Uncle Thing, Bug, and Fright. Everyone used them. My grandmother said she had two grandchildren and a disgrace. I was the sauce stain on the wedding dress, the fly in the ointment, the hair in the soup.

Sometimes my mother started on the clear liquid at eleven in the morning, in her robe, with a

Virginia Slim clasped between her teeth. Her ritual at the kitchen table involved serving herself a shot, downing it, leaning forward, taking a deep breath, squeezing an orange, drinking the juice, thinking for a few moments in silence, and then pouring herself another shot of tequila, squeezing another orange, drinking the juice, and thinking again. She'd turn around and explain herself to me, probably while I was eating or doing my homework:

"I need to hydrate."

But then the assault began: you were born ass-first, my pussy looks like a frying pan, you're good for nothing, you don't have a vocation, and no one can survive without a vocation, you never dress up, you walk around like a lesbian, in those baggy sweatshirts, with your hair like that, you think that's modern? I'm not happy to be your mother, when are you going to get out of this house and leave me alone?

When I started my job renting out my body, my charms, my lovely copper curls, my middling cultural sensibility, and my ass sculpted by years of dancing to Boney M. in my room, my family let up a bit. So it was a good deal for all concerned, you might say. When people see that you're busy, they respect you more.

I told my mother that I was dating Marcio Cafferata (another benefit of the deal) and her jaw dropped.

"I thought he was a little strange...Well, what do you know? This is a pleasant surprise."

She started picturing herself planning a wedding, organizing lunches, drawing up the plans for my future house. Really savoring the candy of having grandchildren with the surname Montegroso Cafferata and all that came with it. Marcio pissed himself laughing when the true scope of our scam dawned on us. Sometimes, we felt sorry for them and murmured, "Our poor parents," in unison. Then we remembered what monsters they were and again, almost as if we'd planned it, would add, "But they deserve it."

My brother saw me coming back home with all these new dresses I was buying at the Galería Precedo and got on the case.

"What are you up to?"

"Nothing."

"Where are you getting the money from? You take a taxi to the gym. It's three blocks away."

"I earn a good wage. I don't have to pay rent. I don't pay taxes. I don't pay for my food. And I'm dating a rich guy."

On Christmas Eve, for which Marcio was the guest of honor, he took me out into the garden to talk to me alone, continuing the role of concerned older brother. I wasn't going to tell him, not yet.

"I'm not into anything shady, don't worry."

"You're dealing drugs."

"No! I can't stand junkies."

"You're fucking a congressman."

"No."

"A senator."

"No."

"An old millionaire."

"No. I'm not going to tell you because I don't want anyone stealing the idea. But it's all legal, don't worry about that."

My poor brother, if only he knew how often I dreamed about fucking him...

Of course, two or three months into our arrangement, I ended up falling in love with Marcio. I couldn't help it. He was the closest person to me in the world, and we knew all about each other's foibles and manias. We knew what made each other tick. Our likes and dislikes were almost exactly the same; we could spend all day watching neorealist movies and eating pizza and the boundaries got blurred. But I'd never ruin a gig like that in a fit of emotion, by making a claim. I embalmed the little bird of love, put it in a glass case next to my other decorations, and had more fun than ever. And I wasn't the kind of person who got carried away with love. I think that can be a little...tacky. As Pedro Lemebel says, "Love is so common, even bums fall in love."

And I wasn't wrong. A year and a couple of months on, Marcio informed me that he was no longer in need of my services; everyone had swallowed the story about our relationship. What could be more credible than a breakup? We agreed to put on a memorable scene at his favorite restaurant to make sure it stayed etched in everyone's minds. We chose a night when plenty of his cousins would be there, their number including bankers, eminent neurologists, and hoteliers. We hadn't yet gotten to dessert when I started to raise my voice and bark back answers to whatever nonsense Marcio had to say, earning my spotlight. I made the scene of my life and even broke a couple of plates, playing it properly unhinged.

"You cheated on me with that bitch! I knew it! I knew it! You cheated on me in front of everyone!"

Marcio could barely stop himself from giggling when he saw me going for broke. I threw a glass of soda in his face and left the restaurant screaming, "What the fuck are you looking at? Haven't you ever seen a jilted woman having a breakdown before?"

The whole thing had been my idea. I thought that, in addition to making it clear that he was heterosexual, it might be a good idea to spread the rumor that he was a Don Juan. Marcio spoke to other friends in the same situation. He told them that I'd saved his life. My name started to spread among the elite of sarcophagused, not closeted, faggots, feeling the pressure of their huge inheritances, pristine surnames, and appearances that mattered more than life itself. Marcio invited me to meetings with potential clients; we met during the buildups to what I was sure were going to be Roman orgies, which I'd have so loved to attend, even if I just stood in the corner and no one touched a hair on my head.

Shortly after our breakup, Marcio called me.

"Do you remember my friend Lao Lavorere? His dad's the director of the Hamilton Clinic? Well, his grandma's coming over from Belgium. She's an old millionaire and he needs to introduce her to a girlfriend, otherwise there'll be consequences."

"What kind of consequences?"

"Rich people problems. The will, probably. But do you remember Lao or not?"

"I don't remember your friend, but I don't care."

"He only needs you for a weekend. He'll pay a lot more than I did and you owe me a night out as a finder's fee."

"How much?"

"Whatever you want."

"Tell him I want a thousand dollars and a white gold ring with a turquoise setting," I said, trying my luck.

"A turquoise, don't be so gauche."

"You just tell him."

Three days later, I had my ring, the thousand dollars deposited in my account, and a date with Lao to get to know him as best I could. We made up a story about where we met, how, who introduced us, what we did on our first dates, the films we saw together, the places we visited, the meals we'd enjoyed, even where we'd touch and kiss one another. At home I recited everything Lao had told me until I had committed it to memory. To flesh out the story, I told him we ought to take some photos. We had to go to an estate near San Javier. Lao's parents were holding a dinner that would be attended by senators, celebrities, journalists, and powerful businesspeople. Even the Riojan would be there...I still can't say his name even though I know he's long dead...I'm superstitious.

Lao and I got along; he was easy to be with as we mingled and smiled. It wasn't a problem kissing him in front of his parents or his grandmother Marie, our Belgian guest of honor.

After that night, it seems that Lao spread the word, because offers kept coming. I was surprised by just how many fags there were lurking in the shadows. They were like an enormous repository of repressed emotion, huge compactors of authenticity, but they were nice too. Encircled by the thorns of appearances, they nonetheless managed to be smart and friendly.

I gave myself the luxury of being able to pick and choose. I would tap my network of gossiping fairies and find out whether the person in question was fun or nice. A few times, the underground lines of communication got it wrong, but I'll get to that later. Once I got the deposit for a month's work in advance, I would study them and decide on the kind of girl-friend that suited them best. I was always a different girl. Even though I used my real name and my life never changed—I still had my two crazy parents and my little job at the newspaper—each of the girl-friends I created was unique. In time, I learned that I couldn't dedicate more than six months of my life to these relationships, the way I had with Marcio. I'd get bored and start to lose focus, to make mistakes in our conversations and secretly begin to hate them. As much as they paid, as good as they smelled, and as fun as they were, by the six-month mark their demands, lives, and whatever situation it was that required my services would begin to wear on me. Of course, it was exhausting. I had to study their lists of acquaintances, relatives, guests at parties, so as not to repeat myself, to avoid mistakes, so I wouldn't go about telling people I was several guys' girlfriend at once.

What kind of profession was this? Was I an actress? A Western geisha? An immaculate prostitute? Was it all a bed of roses? No. I got a couple of nasty fags after whom I had to go to medicine women to rid myself of their bad mojo. Listen, I respect the closet. For many of my friends, the closet was the only safe place they had. But it can be very bad for some fags. They get moldy in there.

Fortunately, I only put up with the first nasty fag for any length of time. It was easier with the others. The moment the tragic fairy warning signs appeared, I tore the relationship out by the roots.

The first was harder because I was determined to be a professional. I refused to let his venom and resentment affect my performance as a girlfriend for hire. But it was impossible to be with someone like that. His irony cut like a saw and his envy ate him up inside. He was a compulsive liar and even accused me of stealing from him, as if it was possible to steal something from that enormous, rotten old maid's house where he'd made his nest like the snake he is. He'd say horrible things about the people he called his friends. And almost five months into the gig, I quit. I told him that I couldn't take any more of the Teatro San Martin ballet, the opera, or anything else from another century, that his breath stank like rotten salami, and I wouldn't work with him anymore, whatever he tried to pay me, because he was unbearable. And after that he spread a rumor about me being a thief.

The funniest job I had was when I was hired to be a lover, not a girlfriend. I was supposed to be the lover of a gay man who had been married for twenty years to a woman who was making his life miserable. He wanted to see if he could get her to catch him with a lover and leave him over it. When he hired me, he didn't say a word about my being part of a love triangle. I started playing the thirtysomething girlfriend of a fiftysomething man without a clue about what was really going on. We started to see each other, to meet in cafés, and sometimes went to hotels in the city center. I was completely oblivious to the fact that someone was taking pictures of us. Someone sent by his wife. We didn't last a month. One night we were having dinner in an Arabic restaurant in the Cerro de las Rosas when a force out of nowhere grabbed me by the hair from behind. Belly dancers swayed around me while the guy's wife gave me the beating of my life. My stomach still hurts when I remember it. She wore herself out kicking me with her Ricky Sarkany stilettos. But the guy didn't move a muscle.

He was more scared than I was. The belly dancers had to carry me out. The supposedly cheated party was arrested and I had to make a statement at the police station. I was covered in bruises, scratches, bites, and cuts. My temporary boyfriend said that he'd pay compensation, asking me to forgive him, he had no idea his wife was capable of that, but if the ploy worked he'd be grateful to me forever.

When I limped back home after making my statement at the station, I told my parents that someone had tried to rob me but I didn't want to talk about it because I had a headache. I locked myself in my room in the dark and went to find something to eat after everyone had gone to bed. A week later, I left. I had enough money to get out of that hellhole.

When his wife finally asked him for a divorce, the disingenuous client paid me extra for the beating, an extremely generous payment that I put toward the apartment where I'm now writing this tale. Two months later, I came across him in Hangar 18 kissing a German exchange student, finally enjoying life out of the closet.

It's thanks to my job as a girlfriend for hire that I first got to see the sea, was able to smell rich people's perfume, and learned secrets that could ruin entire families. I got to see Björk play in Cambridge, swam in the springs of the Mexican Caribbean, and celebrated the New Year on a beach in Ibiza just a few feet away from the abs of Brad Pitt. I spent memorable nights with genuinely wonderful guys, whom I held in the palm of my hand, guys who looked at me with plenty of affection, regardless of the professional nature of our connection. At the end of the day, they were the best kind of relationship. Dancing, laughter, spending hours in a bar waiting for someone they knew to come in, drinking, and kissing their mouths. Mouths like recently plucked damsons. I'd made a fortune as a very special kind of high-end courtesan; I had made sure to disappoint my parents again and again, to keep the bonds that tied us writhing like elegant serpents.

The girlfriend-for-hire gig, rent-a-girl, hologram girlfriend, girlfriend by the hour, unsatisfied prostitute, beard, is over. I fell out of demand. When things got better for the gays, I wasn't needed anymore. The relationships grew ever more seldom and one day I just disappeared.

Occasionally, I stop by to observe my mother's ritual with the tequila and the orange juice, to watch her thinking about who knows what. I feel like telling her what I've been doing all these years, when she thought I was doing nothing at all. Sometimes I feel like going into my father's study and telling him about each of the fake boyfriends I had in secret, whom I introduced to him as the future fathers of my children. But it's a secret that fills me with nostalgia and it wouldn't be right to share that with him. You never know what horrible things a parent might do to your memories.

THE HOUSE
OF COMPASSION

I

The Córdoba pampas. To the south.

The vista is flat and depressing. The horizon, the roads, the deathly smell of pesticides sprayed over the fields, the fathomlessly melancholy, elongated sky, which never gets quite blue enough. The trucks cruelly speeding by. And also, impossible to ignore, the proximity of the city not so many miles away.

But right now, we're concerned only with the pampas. A gas station, the wind blowing resolutely unchecked, and a few parked cars. Some are filling their gas tanks, others are getting something to eat, some just need to use the bathroom. You won't find many clean bathrooms around here.

A small car, a red Ford Ka carrying a small family—mom, dad, and a girl—slows down.

"I told you to go before we left," the mother scolds the child, furious because now she's going to have to set foot in a bathroom that, as we've already established, is bound to be filthy.

"Yes, Ma, you told me a hundred times. Shouting about it won't help."

The mother has slammed the door shut and is heading for the door with an "L" for "Ladies."

"Then you can go in on your own, I'll be out here, smoking."

The girl rushes inside and opens a cubicle barely big enough to fit a toilet. She pees desperately.

"Don't touch the toilet, don't touch the bowl, for goodness' sake!"

A shiver of relief runs through her. Oh, what a lovely feeling! Someone flushes in the next-door cubicle. It's a good thing she's still holding in that fart. What if someone heard? A sweet perfume floats over from the other side of the tiled wall.

She dries herself from front to back with a piece of toilet paper the way her mom showed her and goes straight out to wash her hands. The woman is standing with her back to her. She's wearing high-heeled boots and a very short miniskirt and has slender, toned legs. She's very tall. And so skinny! The girl likes her makeup, the kind you see in science fiction movies, colors glittering all over. It sparkles more when she shakes out her hair.

"Would you like to wash your hands?"

The girl nods shyly, terrified. She's not tall enough to reach the tap. The woman's voice is metallic, nasal, the voice you'd expect from a travesti. *Is she...? Maybe she... Oh... I'll die if I've met a real travesti. Die, die, die, wait until the girls at school hear about this. If Mom comes in now, I'll die. She's got lipstick on her teeth. Should I tell her? No, don't say anything, she'll see when she checks herself in the mirror.*

"Would you like some soap?"

The girl nods again and cups her hands underneath the dispenser, which is also out of her reach.

The travesti's hand is large and hairy, like a dog's paw.

"What's your name?"

"Flor," she answers as she continues to smear on her lipstick. As though she didn't have plenty on already. She rubs her stained teeth with her finger.

"I'm Magda."

"That's a nice name. What are you doing here?"

"We're going to my grandmother's wake in Córdoba. We're coming back tomorrow night. My mom's angry."

"Because she has to go to Córdoba?"

"No, she didn't want to come by car because of the accidents."

The travesti turns off the faucet, grabs some paper towels, and hands them to her to dry her hands.

"Want to know my full name?"

The girl nods again.

"My name is Flor de Ceibo Argañaraz."

And, as though trying to change the subject after her revelation, she adds:

"You have beautiful eyes. I love their color. I recognize the gleam I had when I was your age."

Time appears to have stopped. They can't hear the trucks, or the cars Dopplering by. It's as though the whole pampas has disappeared.

"You know where that gleam comes from?"

The girl shakes her head and fixes a pair of eyes that look fit to burst on the woman.

"Fear of grown-ups. You know? Don't you think grown-ups are scary?"

"Oh."

"Aren't you ever scared of grown-ups?"

"Yes, sometimes. But I also feel sorry for them."

"Sorry?"

"Yes, I feel bad for them. My friends and I are always saying how we feel bad for our parents."

She's a feisty little one. Intelligent and feisty.

"You're right to be scared of grown-ups. I used to be like you, my eyes gleamed."

"Can I ask you a question without you getting upset?"

"Of course, honey, nothing upsets me."

"Are you a travesti?"

"Yes, and one of the most authentic ones you're likely to find around here. One hundred percent travesti."

"When I tell the girls at school, they won't believe it…"

Magda's mother's knuckles rap on the metal door. She's just finished her cigarette and remembered that she has a daughter.

"Come on, Magda! What are you up to in there? Hurry up, your father's waiting for us in the car."

"Go. And remember: ceibo blossom is our national flower. Maybe you'll think of me someday."

The moment she's out, her mother locks her in a vise-like grip and marches her back to the car.

"Magda, were you talking to someone?"

"No, I was singing. What's a national flower? Like the queen of flowers? Which is Argentina's national flower?"

"How should I know? Where did that come from?"

The father has bought sodas and chips at the store. The wind is corrosive and persistent enough to make you suicidal. The girl in the back seat is already drinking her Coke.

"Put on your seat belt."

The mother swallows her chips and looks out at the road stretching ahead of her. The father starts the car and just as it's moving off, a big dog steps out in front and turns to look at them. Magda screams:

"Stop, Daddy! You're going to run it over!"

"You see? I told you, this road is dangerous."

The dog doesn't move until the girl holds a chip out the window. It comes over and leaps up onto the door. The mother screeches in fright. The animal takes the chip delicately from Magda's hand.

"Come on, let's go before the dog gets in with us!"

The car pulls out and disappears down the road.

II

Now we see Flor de Ceibo coming out of the bathroom. She's stumbling from side to side. Maybe the girl didn't notice how drunk she was, or maybe she just ignored it. There goes this splendid example of womanhood in her silver Lurex miniskirt, short enough for her and her alone, and her weathered boots with the heel bent back but still roadworthy. They even have a kind of refinement. Underneath the jean jacket she altered and cut the tassels off herself, she's wearing a top that barely covers her hormone-induced breasts. "Men don't see these things. They don't know how to appreciate them. You could have a peacock sticking out your ass singing in Mandarin and they'd barely notice. You dress for yourself, that's how it is, that's why you're a travesti," an old travesti said to her once in La Piaf, a gay dive that was both her school and her paradise.

Flor de Ceibo has had a long night. She saw to six johns. The sun hits her face. She looks in her handbag for her sunglasses but can't find them. There's not a shadow to be found in the pampas. "You need to settle down. Go to Rosario. There, the guys go nuts over queens, out here on the road if you're not killed by a farmer, you'll be hit by a car," the same travesti said to her on another occasion. "There, when you stick out your ass it never touches the ground. These guys fuck you in midair. Listen to me. One weekend a month. You'll come back fucked by a bunch of bull *chongos* and rolling in money. Then you can give it all to that idiot you live with."

Flor de Ceibo considers her friend's advice. Things have been pretty ugly around here recently. Johns don't want to pay what she's asking and she has to work more to make the same money she used to from just two or three guys. They too are afraid of hitting an animal crossing the road and ending up a shrine surrounded by empty bottles and plastic flowers. It's time to make a move, try her luck in Rosario. Flor's grown tired of this fucked-up pampas highway routine.

But today that routine has a twist. In addition to meeting that girl, Oh, what was her name, María, Marta, Mar...Magda, that was it, from the Bible...something else is going to happen.

A group of nuns is walking toward her on the other side of the road. They're from the Order of the Sisters of Compassion. They're amusing themselves, clinging on to their habits, which billow out and threaten to fly off when a car passes by. Flor de Ceibo stares at them, fascinated by how the light glints off their hoods and the laughter of nuns tempted by what the wind is doing beneath their rebellious skirts. Their legs are quite hairy, she notices at a gust of wind. Of course, nuns don't shave. They're looking back at her too. They bless her, smiling. One of them raises her hand in farewell. She's a young nun, maybe about fifty. She has a smile as wide as the pampas horizon, tooth after tooth stretching on forever. Flor de Ceibo smiles back, a little self-conscious about her missing premolar, and she thinks she sees a thick strand of drool dripping down the side of the nun's smiling face. A nun with false teeth? She doesn't trust them, no reason to deny it. But right now, she's fixated on the smile. What do they have underneath their habits, in addition to the hairy legs? Flor pictures gigantic bloomers and iron chastity belts.

She turns several times to keep her eyes on the nuns. The nun who waves at her turns too. Now they're running. "I think she likes me," Flor de Ceibo says to the other Flor de Ceibo inside, whom she's been talking to for years. There aren't many other people with whom she can have such sincere, entertaining conversations.

She turns down a dirt track that circumnavigates a soccer field, walks on about a hundred and fifty feet, and she's home. She opens the door and the metal scrapes against the concrete. The house groans. But it's a pretty house; flowers grow in the beds she waters every morning when she gets back from work. Snapdragons, begonias, hibiscus, busy lizzies, pansies, and geraniums. The façade is painted a very pale yellow and from the outside you can see the thick curtains she cut and sewed herself. An autumnal motif with neatly stitched hems and ruffles.

The entrance is a cement path with a stone surface she painted in every color that came to her in cast-off tins of paint. The only note out of place is the stone box containing the electricity meter where someone has spray-painted CHRIST IS CUMING in black. She should cover it up with something colorful but right now she doesn't have the money to rid herself of the apocalyptic warning.

She puts her handbag down on the table, takes off her boots, and kicks them into a corner. Then she goes back out and picks up the hose already connected to a faucet at the entrance and waters the plants, humming a tune. Once the earth has turned a milky coffee color, she turns off the faucet and rolls up the hose.

Now she heads into the bedroom. She pulls back the curtain, which she stitched herself as well, and the first thing she sees is a prone man. Her uncle has made himself at home, watching television as if he owned the place, lost in his cartoons. On the nightstand is a mug of coffee and the sheets are covered in crumbs, meaning that once again he's ignored instructions to eat in the kitchen. She takes off her clothes and lets them fall to her feet. Her uncle doesn't look at her; his only reaction is to alter his breathing a little. He's about sixty, with a thin, pointy chest like the prow of a boat.

"Fucking hell. I forgot to take off my makeup."

She gets up with a sigh and goes to the bathroom to smother her face in cold cream. When she gets back, she looks miraculously younger. We have no way of knowing whether she knows that the makeup ages her. Maybe no one's ever told her but like this, with her face bare, she definitely looks a lot younger. Now the uncle acknowledges her presence. He licks a finger and shoves it between her buttocks. She swats him away like an annoying fly.

"Stop it. Leave me alone."

"Huh...we'll see," says the old man before turning back to his cartoons.

Sometimes it's as though the heat takes a break and then the uncle's sweat dries on his skin and he gets cold, so he hugs her again. She pushes him away irritably and, naked as the day she was born, she goes out to the garden to lie on a lounger.

The uncle, alone in the bedroom, travels back in time. He sees his nephew come in through the front door. A timid kid goat, already lost in the world, small bones, straight jet-black hair. They dropped him off the same day that his sister died. He barely spoke. No more than yes, no, and uh-huh.

It was easy. He'd get back home from driving the taxi he had back then and sit him on his lap to watch cartoons together. He arranged his nephew's body as best suited him. He started stroking his knees, almost by accident, carelessly, until his stroking relaxed the boy's muscles and one afternoon he lay back on his chest. The boy's neck was very close to his mouth and so he started to kiss his ears, as if it was a joke. He saw goose pimples form all over the boy's skin. He kissed him on the mouth, his tongue probing as though it was looking for a wellspring, until it found one. After that he made him wash his shit-stained underwear and hit him every time he felt that life was unfair. It was a long, languorous crime, committed patiently.

Did that boy have bright eyes like Flor de Ceibo said a moment ago to the girl in the gas station bathroom? In the images bouncing around the uncle's head you can't see very well, so we'll never know. But you must always believe people like her, even when they're not telling the truth.

One day, the nephew decided to paint his nails a pearly white and his skin began to smell of Hinds cream and Impulse deodorant. His uncle invited him to sleep with him. In the warm embrace of field-toughened arms, the pubescent flower slept with one eye open every night until his fears faded. He allowed his uncle in and the man shoved deep enough to touch his belly button. Flor de Ceibo fell in love and regarded the incestuous relationship as a romance, with all the associated jealousy and petty squabbling. When money grew tight, she went out onto the street to make a living; at the end of the day, it was a worthy profession. She headed out to the road where she'd seen other travestis ply their trade and stuck with them. By the end of the first night, the same blood beat in her too. She was making her own money and could treat herself to things her uncle never gave her, like white coffee with *medialunas* in the morning and Coca-Cola every day. She took a bus into the city and bought herself some clothes, and before long she was surrounded by guys desperate to make love to her in cheap but convenient motels. Her uncle grew lazy and sold the taxi. His belly grew and his teeth fell out. His frame became frail and his blond Córdoba-gringo hair turned dry and yellow. Flor was no longer willing to see to his needs in bed and she began to choke on the stench of poverty. She divorced him in secret. Around then she began to come to the realization, thanks to her friends on the road, that her uncle had used her for years. She cursed him in her own language, inside, with feeling. She stayed with him, but she made him pay for the shit he put her through with her heartfelt disdain.

Flor de Ceibo sleeps on the lounger, which she moves around, following the sun, so tired that she doesn't see a pair of children spying on her from the roof of the house next door. When the sun abandons the garden, she goes back inside and finds her uncle drinking maté tea and watching the afternoon soap, the one with the worst actors.

"Just like a woman, what do you know…" she murmurs as she passes by.

The uncle is still in his TV-induced stupor. It's time: she drinks skimmed yogurt straight from the pack, downing about a pint without taking a breath. The she gets into the shower, soaps herself, shaves her legs, buttocks, and crack until they're smooth as a gravestone. She dries herself off. Rubs in cream. The uncle sees her shrouded in a cloud of steam. She puts on the skimpy clothes we saw her wearing in the morning.

"Be careful, there are plenty of crazies out there."

"You're telling me…I've got their king right here."

"I mean it. And now to cap it all off, the fucking dogs have started crossing the road. There's a crash every other day. The cars turn over trying not to hit the animals. The side of the road is covered in crosses."

"When I need a father, I'll find one who doesn't want to fuck me, you dirty old man."

The uncle stands up, ready to give her a beating, and her initial reaction is fear but then she composes herself and her corrosive smile returns.

"Do it," she goads him. "Do it and see if you ever get a good night's sleep again. I'll burn the fucking house down with you and everything else in it."

As his niece leaves him in the house alone and depressed, watching the soap, his manhood in shreds after his failed attempt at physical abuse, he picks up the towel she used to dry herself and masturbates angrily, squeezing his cock until it spurts a sticky, stinky gray liquid into the fabric.

III

Flor de Ceibo at work.

Queen of careful drivers. They're afraid of the dogs who've taken to stepping out in front of cars and causing accidents. The animals have grown adept at leading souls into next world.

Strong legs and hands, capable of strangling a bulky trucker, should the need arise. She begins her night like an actress in a play. She rations her energy. She knows there's no reason to use it all up in the first encounter. She can last all night without having to spend it hanging around the trucks. Summer nights are easy to bear.

"If you're smart, it won't take longer than seven minutes. Just say, Yes, papito, and grope their package and you'll have them ready to burst. You need to keep an eye on the time. Soon enough, you'll be amazed by how quickly the money rolls in." Advice the travestis gave her when she started out.

Now a pair of johns beckon her over from a car with flashing blue lights, like a police cruiser. She's already seen off one in half an hour and cleaned herself up as best she could in the gas station bathroom. Now she sashays through the night like a snake with hair instead of scales.

Following the requisite negotiations, the three lovers take a car to a motel not far away. The Traveler's Kiss is its name and it is extremely popular with the local travestis and the few couples who slip away to the remote corner of the planet where this story is set. The boys are simple, they don't say much, they're not curious about her. They talk about the weather, the latest traffic accident: an animal that the specialists haven't yet identified, a kind of dog with long legs, was hit by a car.

Flor de Ceibo is bored, her mind elsewhere, on the nun who waved to her that morning on her way home. The men drone on and on but she's still pondering the nuns' hairy legs, and the one bathed in the morning light who smiled so sweetly with drool running down the side of her mouth.

Her eyes fill with tears that she'd never be able to explain to her johns if they asked, so she brings a nail hardened by layer after layer of varnish and flicks them out the window. The earth burns and vegetation shrivels where they fall.

They get to the motel, settle on a price for the room, get undressed, mess around, and come and go between the different bodies. Light from the neon arrows pointing the way into the temple of sex by the hour slips through the gaps in the curtain. From her queenly throne, with a small but broad foot she strokes the bodies of farm boys raised on fresh milk and homemade bread while they squeeze her bitch tits, calling her little whore, lovely whore. Flor de Ceibo likes one of them, the younger one. He's tall and well built. And nice too. The kind of country bumpkin you want to take away to a cabin in the mountains and force to work the land naked. The kind you want to tell you love while you bite on his peachy nipples. Straight but beautiful.

The other one shoves his cock in her mouth and grabs the back of her head, pushing until she gags, making her feel as though she's fucking a washing machine. Or a chest of drawers.

"Everything all right?" he asks.

"Yes, fine. You don't like how I do it?" Flor de Ceibo asks innocently as though she were thinking about something else entirely. The john's question reminds her of her business. She's picked up a pair of pampas farm boys on the road and now she needs to see to them like the professional she is.

"We'll see, do it and I'll let you know."

Flor de Ceibo does what she has to do, but she's distracted. What's she doing thinking about those nuns she saw that morning?

It drags on, it looks as though they'll take a while to come. This could last for hours. Fortunately, the agreed-on price was by motel hours; they'll have to either pay up or keep a better eye on the time.

She has some well-proven theories in the field of hurrying orgasms. A girl like her is ready to use every trick in her toolbox. For example, talking to them like a little girl makes them come faster. Baby talk, they call it these days. If she starts to moan and pout, the orgasm comes. It works on a lot of them and she's honed her technique at getting them hot and bothered. If they're extremely slow, a finger in the ass always tips the balance in her favor. None of her johns having difficulty spilling their load has been able to resist her finger. A little shuffle and that's it. *Let's see if the theory still holds*, she thinks, and wets her middle finger ready to shove between the buttocks of the guy she doesn't like so much so she can finish him off quickly and move on to the guy she prefers. It's not mala praxis but as she proceeds, maybe because her nail is too long, or because she didn't wet her finger enough, when she, concentrating on the blow job, plunges her finger in his ass, the boy hits her in the head, a little above the temple, knocking her over, surprised and indignant.

"Hey, don't hit her," says the other one. "I don't want any trouble with the tranny."

"She tried to shove her finger in my ass, the faggot."

"Don't hit her, or there'll be trouble."

Flor de Ceibo gets back up, still a little dazed. She looks for something to hold on to but can't find anything and falls back down. Finally, she manages to get upright and the three of them are silent, sizing each other up as they try to decide what to do next. It's one of those times when you can cut the air with a knife, which is how she plans to describe it to her friends when it's over. The johns are scared when they see Flor de Ceibo sway. You could hear a pin drop. Little by little she steadies herself and in the blink of an eye she leaps onto the body that hit her and sinks her teeth into his shoulder. They're a pair of well-built men, but they can't pull her off.

When she lets him go, she sees her johns staring at her in terror. She knows that they need to be afraid of her if she's going to get them to do what she wants.

"Give me your money and his, the cell phones and watch," she says. She reaches into her handbag and takes out a knife that gleams like an ice cube, brandishing it decisively so they know just how dangerous she is.

"Leave me my ID," begs one of the johns.

"I'm giving you back your wallet."

She gets dressed quickly, without taking her eyes off them. She's wet with their saliva; her underwear is damp. And just like that, as if nothing has happened, she withdraws from the stage, gracefully, under the worried gazes of the johns who just happened to pick her up that night.

"Wait fifteen minutes before leaving. There are cameras in the room. The motel staff know me. If you try something, they'll defend me."

"We'll meet again," threatens the one she bit.

As she leaves through the motel entrance, she passes one of the cleaning women smoking a cigarette.

"What did you do, Flor?" she asks.

"I didn't do anything."

She takes out a tissue and wipes the blood from her teeth and lips. All that biting messed them up.

When she does these robberies, the adrenaline gets her higher than marijuana, it's better than ecstasy and alcohol. She'd feel guilty, only she's a travesti. She works on the road; guilt isn't for creatures like her. Her lot is to stretch out in the sun, cover herself in Hinds cream and Impulse deodorant, and make her uncle sick with desire. It's to match anyone who attacks her blow for blow, simply, honorably. It's easy to deal with the police. There isn't a policeman alive who doesn't lust for travesti flesh. It's spells, sticking pins into dolls and putting curses on houses. Travestis have done well to sow fear with their spells on the homes of those who abuse them. The gremlin of fear passes from mouth to mouth like a kiss. Flor de Ceibo is protected by the trench she did her part to dig.

IV

Flor de Ceibo walks confidently down the side of the road. She spins like a model on the catwalk when a passing car honks its horn. But the car belonging to the boys she's just robbed swerves off the road and parks on the shoulder in front of her. Flor de Ceibo runs into the fields and disappears into the soybeans.

She runs in her weathered heels, hears people swearing at her from behind, her attackers getting closer. She runs farther and farther through the fields like a fox up to no good, followed by maligned, robbed, and humiliated men. Now it's corn, tall corn golden like in Flor de Ceibo's dreams, it hides her from pursuers ready to beat the shit out of her for what she did to them, a pair of decent kids who didn't do anything wrong.

The moon is white and pale and Flor de Ceibo's steely legs start to wobble. She collapses. When the boys see her fall, they approach with caution. While she lies lifeless on the ground, they decide to search through her handbag to get back their cell phones, money, and anything else she might have on her.

"Let's go, we don't want to get caught up in anything," says the short-tempered farm boy.

"We should let someone know," says the other one.

"Leave her for the jackals."

V

Flor de Ceibo opens her eyes. She's in a cool room, so cool she's not hot even under all these blankets and sheets so white they blind your eyes. They smell good. The floor is wooden cobbles and the low ceiling has beams running along it. It smells good in the room; the walls are redolent with whitewash and women's secrets. From the bed, Flor de Ceibo sees a large wooden rosary dangling by her head. One of her eyes hurts, it feels swollen. She brings her hand to her forehead and finds that it's bandaged, swollen all around her eyebrow. The pristine white pillowcase is a relief map of blood but she can't see that right now.

All she remembers are a few scratches running through the corn field. She must have bumped her head when she fell. Her hearing begins to return, bringing her the sound of something like a dog panting underneath her bed. She leans over as best she can to look but nothing's there. She can still hear breathing.

The door opens. One of the nuns she saw on the road tiptoes in.

"Are you awake?"

"Where am I?"

"At the convent of the Sisters of Compassion. We found you last night at the bottom of the garden. We decided not to let anyone know before you woke up, just in case."

The nun leaves and we hear her call down the corridor.

"Sister Rosa! She's woken up!"

Now the barking rings out loud and clear, accompanied by exclamations of joy from other nuns. The door opens again and the nun who smiled at her on the road yesterday morning comes in. Behind her comes the sound of more nuns' footsteps. A very young, dark-skinned one, as shy as a bunny rabbit, is named Ursula. Another skinny nun, lively as a lizard, curious and sincere, stares at her hardest and introduces herself with a spontaneous kiss on the cheek.

"I'm Shakira."

Flor de Ceibo is a little lost, like she's trying to walk on a waterbed. Did these naughty nuns drug her?

"It's my real name. She was very big when I was born and my mom loved her. She was fourteen when she had me."

Together with Rosa, Ursula, and Shakira is an old woman they call Mother. They speak to each other in unintelligible whispers. It sounds like another language.

Now Sister Rosa sits down on the side of the bed. She's so gentle you couldn't possibly be scared of her. She takes Flor's hand, which has a raw scratch on it, and starts to lick it, running her tongue over the wound again and again.

Ursula offers an explanation:

"Saliva is full of antibodies, it'll do you good."

"My name is Sister Rosa. You're at the convent of the Sisters of Compassion. It's November 24, 2019. The doctor has been to see you. We were worried about that terrible bump on your head. You got five stitches. We knew not to call the police, just in case. A lot of girls like you come by here. We've had girls like you stay two years in a row. Sometimes we hope that they'll take their vows, but none has so far."

After a long pause, she adds, patting Flor's hand: "You're at home here."

The other nuns giggle a little but Sister Rosa barks: "Be quiet!"

"My uncle must be worried," Flor de Ceibo murmurs.

Blurry images come back to her, nuns feeding her, ghostly nuns washing her, praying at her side, talking to her. Nuns with thick, dirty nails from working in the earth. Sister Rosa lying on the ground licking her wounded hand. Sleep reclaims her before she can ask any more questions. All she can do is murmur again that they need to let her uncle know.

She wakes up desperate to go to the bathroom. She tries to sit up but she's very weak. Her legs are skin and bone, as though she'd never walked in her life. She feels something uncomfortable under her nightdress. She reaches down and realizes she's wearing a diaper.

Get up, you faggot, the Flor de Ceibo inside her urges. *Get up, you faggot, come on.* When she does manage to get upright, it doesn't last a second. She falls straight back down.

"Girl, what are you doing trying to get up by yourself?! You should have called me."

How can she call her if she can barely open her mouth? It's as though her tongue has grown much too big for her palate; it feels heavy and disobedient. Sister Ursula helps her into the bathroom and pulls down her diaper. Flor de Ceibo is embarrassed to let the nun see her dick, but Ursula doesn't seem to care.

"I need to poop, can you leave?" Flor says, mustering the last of her strength.

"I can't leave you alone in the bathroom. Don't worry, just go, I'll look the other way."

After trying, her belly refuses to relax.

"I can't."

The nun takes a piece of toilet paper and cleans her penis the way you'd dab at the sides of a baby's mouth. Then she puts the diaper back on and takes her back into the room. The drunken sensation begins to fade.

"I'm a little hungry."

"That's a good sign. A patient who eats is one who survives, my grandfather used to say. It's very true. We'll bring you some breakfast."

"What time is it?"

"Ten-thirteen in the morning. The sun will be coming in through the window soon. Look." She pulls back the curtain for her to see the sun shining down, the light filtering through the lapacho trees, which are in full bloom.

A little while later we see Flor de Ceibo drinking a deliciously sweet white coffee with slices of home-made bread and butter, honey, a pot of fruit salad, a glass of orange juice, and a lapacho flower on the tray. The bread is spongy and light, the water is cool, and there are slices of ham and cheese on a plate.

"How did you find me?" she asks.

"Thanks to the dog. Nené. Our dog. She came looking for Mother Superior making a fuss; it was early, we were praying the rosary for dawn. We went out and saw Nené sniffing you excitedly and we carried you back."

"I was being chased by a pair of disgruntled customers and ran too far. I didn't realize."

"They were chasing you to beat you up."

"Yes. I robbed them, their things are in my handbag."

"They must have taken them, all there was in your handbag was your ID and house keys."

Sister Ursula laughs in a way that makes Flor de Ceibo uncomfortable; the sound unsettles her a little.

She's heard it before. She remembers documentaries about the African savanna, the hyenas cackling around a dead animal.

Flor de Ceibo continues savoring her coffee, which hasn't yet gone cold.

"You can go back to sleep after your breakfast."

"I think I can walk," says Flor de Ceibo.

She stands up. The nun is very close by. She smells like a damp rag. The nun smiles stupidly and as she does a line of drool dribbles down and dangles from her chin. She doesn't seem to notice. Flor de Ceibo loses her balance and sits back down.

"I got dizzy."

On her second attempt, leaning on the nun's shoulder, she takes a few steps. These first few steps in the room in the convent are the beginning of a new story for her, a change in the nature of her suffering. Soon the doors of the convent will open to these steps and she will get to know the layout of the place where she has been cared for.

She walks into in a well-lit kitchen with plenty of appliances on the shelves, a wood-fired pizza oven at one end, and a gas one at the other. There's a two-door refrigerator and a long table with eight chairs on either side. And then through another door a gallery with columns wrapped in ivy and tiny flowers that flutter their yellow petals as though they were alive. And beyond the gallery is a garden with pergolas, damson, peach, apple and lemon trees, dogs playing, cats sleeping in the branches, and gray birds scattered on the grass like seeds and behind it all a vegetable patch with its own character, wilder than the Amazon, as healthy and anarchic as anything she's ever seen.

Flor de Ceibo's paces grow steadier. Sister Rosa is harvesting some green squashes good enough to eat then and there but when she sees her pass by she smiles again, the same way she smiled on the road that morning. Beyond her, Sister Shakira is feeding the chickens, ducks, and turkeys who strut around as if they own the place.

"This is where Nené found you," Sister Rosa tells Flor de Ceibo.

"Is she a nun?" she asks, a little disoriented from the walk and all these dreamlike visions. She thought she saw the oldest nun, the Mother Superior, milking a goat that bleated between each squeeze.

"No, she's our dog," answers Sister Shakira. "Nené! Come here, Nené!"

She hears a good-sized animal shaking herself off in the undergrowth, the moan of a bitch woken early from her nap and the heavy padding of paws.

A little while later a muzzle appears in the low grass, strong, square, and dun-colored, followed by equine haunches. She's tall and dignified. Flor de Ceibo gets a fright when she sees her and falls back onto the soft grass. Nené comes over and sniffs her and for a second Flor de Ceibo Argañaraz thinks she sees her smile.

"Don't be afraid, she's harmless," says Sister Shakira.

Noise comes from the convent gallery. Flor de Ceibo stands up to see what's going on and past the plants and animals she sees a pair of nuns pulling each other's hair on the floor, fighting like ordinary layfolk. They don't wear anything underneath the habit. Just hair and a dark thicket around the pubis. They're separated by the oldest nun, the one they call Mother. She smacks them apart with a rod, shouting for good measure.

Flor de Ceibo can't breathe, she doesn't blink or move a muscle. Nené is close by. Her ferocious-looking muzzle is an inch from her nose. The little nun with the flighty habit has told her that she's a dog but this isn't a dog. It's something else. It's as if it can read her thoughts. Nené steps back and howls like a witch. Then she sneezes and enthusiastically runs off to chase the chickens around the garden.

"Oh, my goodness! What is that?" Flor de Ceibo exclaims.

"They wanted to kill her, we tempted her here with food. She had a brother but he was killed by a farmer," says the Mother Superior on her return from ending the fight.

"She's pregnant, you know," she goes on, helping Flor to her feet with an easy pull that belies her years. Heroic strength. "People don't know what's good for them, they've started to hate them because they say they're satanic. But I say how can a satanic animal be happy living in a convent? We have to keep her from drinking the holy water."

"She was barking at my knees, trying to warn me something was going on," adds Sister Rosa. "She's smart. We need to understand her better but it's almost like how we talk to each other. She stayed by your door all night. When it's hot she likes to sleep inside or out here in the woods."

"Are you tired?" Shakira asks.

"A little, but I'd like to stay out in the sun," says Flor de Ceibo.

Midday comes around and for lunch they have sandwiches of homemade goat's cheese, tomatoes from the garden, and fried eggs. The bread is spread with avocado, also from the garden. It's clear that God loves this convent.

As they enjoy the food, which is accompanied by lemonade, they hear a crash on the road, several hundred feet away. Sisters Ursula and Shakira leave the table and run off to see what happened.

"Nené," says Sister Rosa, jumping up from her chair. "Please, finish your lunch, we need to see what happened."

She goes off calling, "Nené, Nené," but the dog, or whatever it is, doesn't come.

"We're always on tenterhooks," says the Mother Superior. "She's a lovely animal but people don't like her. The farmers are superstitious, as you probably know. They see them in the fields and they start shooting because they're scared. A vet came once and said that they're not domesticated. He told me the name, but I've forgotten. But I can prove to you that they're perfectly tame."

The Mother Superior gets up easily and beckons to Flor de Ceibo, who's very much enjoying her sandwich. "Come with me."

They walk down a cool, clean passage to an ordinary-looking door. The Mother Superior opens it and what appears before Flor de Ceibo's eyes is a garden that isn't the garden she was in that morning. This is even bigger with fewer trees but plenty of roses, and carnivorous angel's trumpets ready to snap up a hummingbird in the blink of an eye. Leaping around everywhere are hundreds of dogs like

Nené. Hundreds of dogs with horses' hooves. They gambol around Flor de Ceibo's legs, threatening to knock her over, but the Mother Superior holds her up with her freakish strength.

"If we don't keep them here, they'll die out," says the Mother Superior as she laughs and coos to the animals, who are happy to see her. "Come on, let's finish our lunch. Tomorrow, if you like, I'll introduce you to them all. They're baptized. I did it myself in the chapel font. If the priest ever finds out, he'll kill me."

They go back to the dining room and finish eating. A little while later Sisters Ursula, Shakira, and Rosa return with sorrowful expressions. Shakira can't stop spinning, as if she's momentarily lost her reason.

"Nené again…she stood in front of a car and it swerved into a milk truck."

"Were there fatalities?" asks the Mother Superior wearily.

"The family in the car. A couple with a little girl."

Flor de Ceibo immediately thinks of Magda, the girl she spoke to in the gas station. Ursula resumes her lunch, lost in thought.

"Do you know what the names of the victims were?"

"No. It was a red Ford Ka. It got messed up."

"What about Nené?"

"We don't know, she ran off across the road. So they said."

"She's alive, otherwise the others would be going nuts," says Sister Shakira.

They take Flor de Ceibo back to her room and let her rest all afternoon. At night, they bring her dinner: vegetable soup with half an avocado in it, sprinkled with lemon juice. To drink there's cold green tea. It's brought by Sister Rosa.

"There's no way we can let you leave."

"Of course you can, I can leave whenever I want," says Flor de Ceibo, emboldened by the food.

"You can't. Nené asked us to keep you. You can't leave."

Flor de Ceibo thinks they're drugging her food. She pushes the tray to the floor and shoves the nun with the maternal smile over a small stool by an antique wooden desk. When she opens the door, the enormous dogs are staring at Sister Rosa, who gets back up, laughing and groaning.

Flor de Ceibo tries to leave but the dogs growl at her, the hair on their flanks bristling. She senses that this isn't something that she'll be able to handle tonight. Sister Rosa's insanely dangerous smile is as bright as the neon sign outside her sinful motel. She goes back to bed and surrenders to sleep while the nun clears away the tray and food.

VI

She keeps asking to speak to her uncle, but the nuns keep coming up with excuses. They sound convincing at the time. It's all she can do to stagger to the bathroom; she doesn't have the strength to resist right now. She wakes up at night determined to find a phone, she's heard one ringing, it must be nearby, but when there isn't a pack of dogs sitting outside her door, the dizziness sends her back to bed.

One morning, she gets to the door to the garden with the dogs and sees her uncle being ripped apart by the beasts. *I hope it's the drugs*, prays Flor de Ceibo as she approaches the carnage. *Let it be the drugs, the drugs.* But it's her uncle, the skinny face, the sunken eyes, the stubble yellowed by tobacco. The dogs growl at each other, jostling to rip a piece of flesh off the body. A hand takes her by the hair and forces her down on her knees. When she looks behind her she sees the outline of the Mother Superior completely naked. She doesn't have a hair on her body.

"I told you that your uncle wasn't answering the phone. Now you know why. He hurt you very badly, Flor de Ceibo, he deserved it. The dogs are just."

VII

On nights of the waning moon, the nuns take Flor de Ceibo out to the second garden, the huge garden patrolled by the dogs, naked. They lay her down on a stone in the night air and draw an inverted cross on her forehead with blood from the Mother Superior's hand. Regardless of the weather. They call Nené, who trots over. The dogs lie down, howling while the nuns perform the ritual. They sing Christian psalms:

God is here today, as certain as the air I breathe,
as certain as the rising sun,
as certain as when I sing you'll hear my song.

Nené jumps onto the stone, stands over Flor de Ceibo's body, and licks her from head to toe with her sandpaper tongue. It tickles Flor de Ceibo terribly but she's usually numbed by the nuns' homemade wine. They drink as if there's no tomorrow before every ritual. She goes happily every time, without a hint of resignation. They treat her like a queen, like a movie star. There, in the night on the sacrificial stone, Nené kisses her all over, her front, her back, every inch. The nuns play the tambourine and sing. She laughs up at the waning moon and lets them. Then, amid hallelujahs and dog stink, she sees Nené stand up and slowly turn into her. Flor de Ceibo. The same hair, the same skin, the same eyes. The Mother Superior hands her the clothes they found her wearing in the cornfield and lovingly helps the new Flor de Ceibo into them.

Every night of the waning moon, Flor de Ceibo Argañaraz sees herself leave the second garden while the nuns sing. She goes straight out to the road. She'd like to warn her johns that it's not her, it's a dog with horses' hooves that causes accidents on the road, just for the fun of it. But she doesn't have the strength to follow Nené, her usurper. She'll escape sometime, when she finds out what kind of order the Sisters of Compassion is and how you get out of there. But it's hard for her to summon the energy: the food is very good and the sheets smell lovely.

COTITA DE LA ENCARNACIÓN

After the torture had commenced, we gave up more than a hundred names. We didn't want to send anyone to the pyre, but the beatings and our fear overcame our will and turned us all into informers. Every betrayal brought more resentment. Eventually, we were gritting our teeth so hard before they were pried open that I ground my molars into dust. Of these hundred names, they crossed the Spanish ones off one by one. They were untouchable. They were pardoned, leaving about fifty prisoners who were crowded into their prison, or that was about the number I counted through eyes swollen from the blows and tears. There must have been just over fifty sodomites locked up in the

cellar for the month and nine days that the perse-
cution lasted. All of us sodomites from the east, Indians, mulattos, and blacks strewn across the floor
like casualties of war. They, foreigners on our soil,
were forgiven in our stead. We told them over and
over again that the absolved Spaniards came to the
east drawn by our song, that they willingly crossed
over to San Pablo, forgetting about the Crown, their
stone churches, and the admonitions of their ancient
books. But it didn't make any difference.

Of the fifty-something detained, no more than
nineteen survived. They died during the interroga-
tions, in the cellar in which they kept us, succumbing
to hunger and thirst, swimming in our own watery
shit and urine bloodied by what they'd done to our
insides. In Mexico, where abundance reigns, where
everything grows and thrives. When there were still
fifty of us, they loosed the hounds, which feasted on
the flesh of those trapped nearest the bars. They
hadn't fed the animals for several days before leading
them down to our cellar. They opened the doors and
undid the locks that bound them. The dogs charged
the sodomites who had been rounded up last, just
after us. Blood leads one to blood like a compass. It
only takes a drop for a river to flow.

The first four, who had renamed ourselves, were
right at the back. The first to be imprisoned. They

found us on the night of September 27, sleeping on top of each other, petrified, in a house we thought would be a safer hiding place. They dragged us out by the hair. I begged them to please drag me from somewhere else; I didn't want to go bald, but they didn't listen. They threw us down there after tying us up like beasts. We were right at the back of the catacomb, skulking in the shadows of our shame.

Juanito Correa, La Estanpa, arrived the day after our detention. She was the first they'd hunted down. She came covered in blood, her face rearranged by their fists. She was missing a piece of her tongue, which she had bitten off during a convulsion while her head was being beaten with a club. And with the tongue she had left, she told me that all of accursed Mexico City was going to fall, that hidden pleasures would be a thing of the past. With the same remnant of tongue, she consoled me for my weakness, for giving up the names of those who had been my friends, lovers, mentors, and greatest loves.

I remember the sun on my buttocks like the eyes of a god, warming my skin. Leaping onto the member of the lover I never heard from again. The high afternoon sun, under willows that covered us with their tears, our rutting echoing out across the salty Texcoco. As I rose and fell on his manhood, I prayed that my guts were clean so as not to ruin the moment with a trace of shit. I liked the lover I had inside of me and he was a virgin. How lucky he was! He was making his debut with the body of the great Cotita de la Encarnación, Juan de la Vega Galindo, the pristine travesti loved by her mother, adored by her neighbors, betrayed by her friend on September 27, in the early days of autumn. I still remember how I spat into the palm of my hand to lubricate our sin before our divine witnesses; the trees, the water, the sun, and the sky. And I remember the giggling we ignored because it was all so lovely between us. We were enjoying ourselves like a pair of animals. But someone was spying on us, someone knew what they shouldn't have known.

Juana, a washerwoman with whom I had washed countless items of clothing on innumerable afternoons, came across our coupling. She ran to the authorities, firing a lightning bolt at my back from her pointed finger. *Juana, you've killed me*, I told her, but she looked down at the ground and the ground looked away. *Juana, you've killed me*, I told her. *Me, who played with your children, who put a cold compress on the forehead of your little Miguelito when the fever was threatening to take him to the boneyard. Didn't I share my maize and chocolate with you? Didn't we laugh together, as friends, standing side by side, when we saw a pair of monkeys fighting over a plantain? Didn't I comfort you when your husband hit you? Didn't I curse him?* But Juana had stopped listening, she had done what she'd done, she had caught us making love like dogs.

You, and you, and you! And you were in my house. You drank the cool water I so generously served, shouted La Estanpa, pointing at each of the priests who came to sprinkle holy water over us. *Let it be known! And that guard standing there, and the one who hit me in the head until my knees shook, you all feasted on my rear as though the world had run out of bread.* But no one was listening anymore, they knew whether she was telling the truth or not, and between them they all came to the understanding that the disgraced women had gone mad. All they did was point their crosses at us. La Estanpa was a woman possessed, cursing all of Mexico. She cursed so hard that her thunder knocked the soldiers to the floor and they went pale with fear.

For a month and nine days they had us locked up in the cellar. We were occasionally visited by very ancient spirits who had learned to speak listening to men gathered around their first fires. At the beginning of everything, when the world was still clean. *Lamashtu, Lamashtu.* Unfathomably old voices who came to remind us that we could still savor the dish of vengeance. *Sink this city, curse it. Dry up the Texcoco.* It was a trustworthy voice, one we'd heard our whole lives. *Lamashtu.* I stood up in disgust after gnawing on the splintered bones the dogs had left behind and condemned the lake where I had washed clothes and made love. *Dry up, swallow this city until not a trace of it remains.*

Before leading us for the first and last time out into the bright Mexican daylight, a short, dirty man came down to the cellar with five soldiers. He was the viceroy's right-hand man, a damned foreigner like the others. He slit the pupils of thirteen of the survivors with a shard of glass. I knew him so well I could name the fleas that hopped around his balls. My hovel knew every side of him, dressed and undressed, elegant and soiled. Maybe that was why he allowed me to keep my beautiful Indian eyes. When he left, sodomite screams and curses echoing in his ears, I bound the thirteen blind fairies with the rags that had survived the dogs' jaws. I kissed their eyes to bury their gazes. La Estanpa screamed that she didn't need eyes, she could see them perfectly well, she remembered their names and she would have her revenge on each of them one day.

Of the nineteen that began the march to the fire, only fourteen made it to San Lázaro, where the lepers lived. The thirteen blind women and myself. We took the first step knowing that plenty of those setting out wouldn't get to burn as we deserved. I remember the orange tongues of flame leaping so high they seemed to be trying to scratch at the clouds with their fiery claws. The wood had retained the violent aromas of the recent summer; it began to drip resin the moment the heat touched it. The sparks prefigured our imminent dance with the devil.

Around us, people laughed and drank wine, they danced and spun as though angels were flashing before their eyes. We, the fallen angels, were shamed in front of everyone. The blind women stumbled, fell, and got back up again. They were clumsy as an axolotl. In the crowd, I saw hands holding stones the size of a human head, sharp spears held high, faces deformed by laughter and screams. Naked, we were a pitiable sight. *Cotita, Cotita, what does flesh taste like?* they shouted. *Juanita Correa, your ass is bleeding, sinner.* Mud formed at our feet, we peed and defecated, a liquid shit, like bird droppings. We were terrified. Many of us cried. Some started to talk in their mother tongue, blind beneath the rags with which I had stanched the bleeding. The language of Indians, the language of our mothers. It was late and on the Zócalo shadows formed crisscrossed by children playing with sticks for swords, killing one another like great lords. The final vision, like a last supper. We said goodbye to the colorful Indian women staring at us fearfully from behind the massed crowd.

They were crying, pulling their shawls around them, and my heart coughed in sympathy, scratching itself from the inside out. I thought about how I would kill them, one by one, how pleasurable it would be to eat my tormentors raw. The men I had loved, who were there now, baying for our blood. The neighbors. Juana Hererra, who had condemned me to this fate. The neighbors who gossiped with such relish about my nighttime affairs. The others. The women whose children I had cared for. Women to whom I gave shelter when their husbands chased them out of their homes. Women whom I bought tortillas and fruit for at the Zócalo, women with whom I shared cuttings from the plants I grew at home. I would have happily killed them all. I had rolled around with all the men throwing filth at us, like the great whore I was, the Siren of Texcoco Lagoon. I had fucked hundreds of these men, I had taught them everything, everything about love, and the only reason I hadn't taught them more was there was nothing left to teach. I taught them to want, to breathe me in from close up, to say nice things and nasty ones. I introduced them to the dirtiness of love, its smell of crap, the rashes and oozing, the pustules, the blisters, and the fevers, the scars and sores, the burning and the bruises that are left after bodies come together. I accustomed them to blood and clean breath from drinking plenty of water and chewing lots of mint, to lubricate with leaf sap, and to eat fruit, while our fornication insulted their god and king. I taught them to forget the shame of being in someone else's hands, naked, with appetites like theirs. I even taught them to make love to their wives. I had eaten them whole, lying in the grass where I slept every night, under banana leaves I had to change after every rainstorm. When they made love to me, it was as though they were swimming in a dark, oily river. I dripped oil like a leaky lamp, they knew the dark shadows between my buttocks, the long night hidden in my ass, the stretched skin of my wrinkles and pits, my straight black hair, sparse from the years I had spent on the earth. They knew every stitch of my doublet, the colored ribbons that fell from my sleeves, the clues I left to guide them to my mouth, hands, and guts. I had given them chocolate to drink. *Your chocolate is delightful, Cotita*, they said. I rubbed my buttocks in burning chocolate and they licked it up. *You mustn't be dirty, Cotita*, they said, and I'd writhe and tell them that the water from this well could be trusted.

Yes, I called those men *my soul, my love*. Of course I did. I was born schooled in the florid ways of romance. My mother washed our clothes at sunset in a pure, gleaming trough. My mother fed me squash flowers when I was sick. My mother was the first to call me Cotita; she rejected the name with which I was baptized. I wasn't Juan to anyone. I called them *my love* and they paid me with a pyre. A long, Mexican love song. I was that too, as well as being a sinner. A poem by Rosario Sansores. A Llorona with a cock who wandered at night among the flowers of the cemetery. A heart that failed beating in the voice of Chavela. The grit of La Doña in the face of the fools who wanted us silent and on our knees. That was who I was then and I didn't know it. On the march, as stones and saliva rained down on us from all sides, I was only sorry for my body.

It wasn't a long walk. They led us at spearpoint. We were close to the pyre now, but inside I went backward, back to when I was a girl and there were no divine powers preventing me from sitting on the ground like the women or cinching my figure with colored ribbons or doubling over when I danced. I saw the blanket my mother embroidered on the day I left home to live my life, very close by, where I rented a hut they set fire to. The house where I danced and sinned and sinned until it was impossible to get out alive. I went so far back—perhaps hallucinating from the hunger that was finally about to come to an end—that I held in my hands, on the path to shame, the blanket my mother gave me when I left. She embroidered a lovely turkey, a brave turkey staring out defiantly, meeting my eye. The eyes that the inquisitor had spared. My eyes, which had seen love in the eyes of many lovers, a kind of transparent stone inside the pupils. Something they wanted to give me, to make earrings with, for my mother to embroider onto my skirts. My eyes, which had played with almost all the children of San Pablo. The eyes of Cotita de la Encarnación, who had cared for and loved other people's children more than their own mothers. I taught them to count and say their prayers in silence, so the angels would protect them and the animal their spirit turned into when they slept would be strong and brave. The children came to my lap, *Auntie Cotita*, they said, making their way past the hens, the dogs, and the goats, the carnivorous plants that stroked them as they went by. They brought me fruit, they filled my lap with fruit. They gave me frogs of every color, *Auntie Cotita, we love you very much.* Their parents knew me, they knew I was honorable, that I'd never hurt anyone or the sacred land of Mexico, the dust of the dead over whom we walked, or the vision of a god in his far-off heaven. The children shouted for joy. They celebrated when they saw my hut burn. They spat too.

I had washed their clothes, I knew what they smelled like up and down and farther down, I had seen all the stains that a body can make. I washed their clothes and dried them in the sun as if they were my own. I dyed their shirts with betel and I smoked out their humors with copal wood. They pushed us toward the pyre, piercing us with their spears. People celebrated as if it was the coming of the New Year. One by one, the sodomites of the city began to burn. The air was soured with their screams and the smell of food, roasted meat. The old people covered their noses with handkerchiefs soaked in wine, which dyed their lips black and their beards violet. They screamed in despair and when their throats were no more, they just burned. The smell of scorched flesh settled in my nostrils, forever blocking out any other aroma.

Finally, I burned. Beforehand, I managed to bite off several ears and they stove in my forehead with a club. It was the fourth or fifth time that I had shat myself in pain. I burned, it lasted forever, to truly know eternity one must be burned at the stake. I wanted to tear myself out of my body, to remove everything that hurt. They kept me in the flames with their spears. And when the pain was gone and everything turned to stars, I saw a woman with the head of a pig. She had cat's claws and a big scar on her belly. I heard my mother's voice singing in Náhuatl. It cleaved to me. I had been torn apart by pain but was made whole again and the woman with the pig's head said to me, *Lamashtu. Stay with your children. Stay with them,*

Lamashtu. It was the same voice that had consoled us in the cellar where we had been imprisoned.

And so I knew that I would be coming back to this world again and again after death. I would commit my goodness to Lethe, I would sip some of the water to forget and return to this world to slip underneath their beds, seed little tumors in their stomachs, their lungs, I would make balls of nails and hair grow in their organs and muscles. I would rain disease down on their descendants, the descendants of all those who found me on September 27, 1658, and those who watched me die in flames a month and nine days later. I would slip my vengeful spirit into the souls of their children. They killed me, so I would take their children. I would take them when they were still children, when they didn't yet know the difference between cruelty and goodness, and in their tiny little bodies I would plant my travesti vice. I would remain in their flesh until they were buried and once dead I would come back and look for another child, grandchild, great-grandchild perhaps, of all those who betrayed me. I would take them at night, change their name and their reflection in the mirror. I would snuff out all hope of seeing them turn into men and scent them with women's oils, imbue them with women's mannerisms. I would cage them in and place deep, deep inside, a terrible hunger for their husbands, generals, presidents, bishops, and popes, for their sons, their brothers, their grandsons, their bosses, and their slaves. Then I'd fuck them all.

When all that was left of the fourteen sodomites who burned in that joyous celebration was ash and charcoal, I cursed these people and filled their lives with minor tragedies. When they threw the remains of the massacre into Texcoco Lake, we began to dry it out. Now, not even its salt remains.

SIX BREASTS

The bird has lost its color. Its tail feathers, which before were red or yellow, are now colorless. It looks as if it's made of saliva. Its song, bitter as a mouthful of shit, sets my teeth on edge out here in the jungle. I write and write. I must write down what happened to us. The days are fraught; each one brings some new natural malice. Nothing is still here, everything is alive, everything scratches, bites, and poisons. I must write, I must, now, at the end of the world. I have my dogs for company and my transparent bird that has craftily shed its color. The days are extremely hot; it's as though I'm seeing everything through a synthetic veil. The iguanas scuttle across the burning sand. Sand that burns my beloved male feet, my enormous feet, with their calluses, bunions, and infections where the worms writhe and lust after one another. In the cool of the night, I pull my wool over me, covering myself as best I can. I clean, cook, and tend to my animals. But I never get time to write. I'm a long way behind what happened but in spite of the delay I write and think about the world I left behind, many lives ago. I must write, from the beginning, to fill the hours in a natural world that is never quiet. It's what my body knows how to do. It is the habit of my hands and mind, a habit from my previous life, when I wrote about films and sometimes literature for a newspaper in the city. The effects of certain books and movies on my life, performances that amazed me, writers who drove me wild, I told the life stories of unforgettable actresses like Carmen Maura and Annie Girardot and those of writers too. I wrote about these things every week and also an aborted novel I left back in my former home. I had a reputation and a wage that allowed me to be happy. I'll just say it: money made me happy.

"This life was won at great cost and they're coming to collect." La Machi sent her chameleon birds to the homes of all the travestis of the city and we, living together blithe and carefree, thought she'd gone mad. La Machi was very old. She'd spent many lives on this earth. We thought she was soon to die and no new Machi had been born to guide the fates of the travestis of our time. "The sky is turning red too early, they're planning a massacre." The chameleon birds arrived at our windows with notes from La Machi tied to their feet. I, for one, just dismissed them as the ravings of an old woman who was threatened by our shared wealth.

I wasn't thinking clearly.

First came Claudia, who said that in one of the houses she cleaned, her boss's cop husband had told her to be careful, not to go out onto the streets alone. Following this advice, she made her *chongo* accompany her every time she left work. The cop hadn't said why, but she'd been scared. Then La Rufiana came over to my apartment, all red from having had to run so far escaping a group of teenagers pelting her with stones. La Machi kept sending her warnings: "Get out of there." The notes tied to the feet of her birds grew ever more urgent. But we were busy spending our money, staying idle to avoid getting wrinkles. Travesti actresses and singers began to be accused on talk shows and news bulletins of being pedophiles or rapists. Then it was the turn of the politicians, the teachers, the journalists, and the writers and soon we all had a sword dangling over our heads. Finally, we heard drones zooming overhead, repeating a slogan in their robot voices:

**DEATH TO ALL TRAVESTIS! AND EVERY-
THING THEY'VE TOUCHED MORE THAN
THRICE. MAKE THE WORLD A BETTER
PLACE. KILL A LITTLE!**

The police shrugged their shoulders. They said that the drones didn't belong to the security forces. We made fun of them, thinking they were the work of religious fanatics. I even laughed at the slogan; they'd borrowed a lovely old line by Jacques Prévert. "So kill a little," "A little trip and one more goes." Whoever wrote the message was a poetry fan.

Posters, radio and TV commercials, street demonstrations, stickers, flyers in schools, preachers in the squares, apparently the whole world was joining in. But neither the government, the army, nor the police had anything to say to us. "We're too busy to open an investigation. Stop pestering us, you shitty women!" The birds kept up their warnings. We thought that if something really serious happened, La Machi would come in person; she'd call a meeting. But the days passed and the damned drones started earlier and earlier and ended later and later:

TO ALL FREE AND DECENT CITIZENS, THE TIME HAS COME TO BRING AN END TO THE DEGENERATION THAT UNDER-MINES THE PEACE OF OUR FAMILIES. KILL A LITTLE. KILL MORE. KILL THE TRAVESTIS AND ALL THOSE THEY HAVE TOUCHED MORE THAN THRICE.

Dying alongside all those we'd touched more than three times. How could you prove something like that? How could they possibly know whether someone had touched a travesti more than three times? Barely a month passed between the day the drones first appeared blaring their message and the first murder. On Instagram the video got millions of likes and people celebrated the deed in the comments section. They'd grabbed a travesti in a clothes store and stuffed her mouth and nose with the clothes she had been trying on until she suffocated. The salesgirls clapped. That day, my son came home from school and locked himself in his room shouting that he was never coming out again, that it was my fault. At his school, signs had been put up that said KILL ALL THE TRAVESTIS AND EVERYONE THEY'VE TOUCHED THREE TIMES. The drones were telling everyone to kill us and we had forgotten the original, transparent violence that we had once used as a defense, the honorable violence that had helped us to endure. One afternoon, I was coming back from work, incredulous at how the atmosphere had changed in just a few days. How people went silent when we passed by, in the street, at the newspaper offices, at the supermarket. They all went quiet and stared at the ground in embarrassment. Suddenly, close to my apartment, four boys stepped into my path. They were in school uniform, backpacks slung from their shoulders. They looked like my son, maybe the same age. They wouldn't let me pass. One shouted that I was a degenerate and threw a stone that hit me on my left side. Then another threw more stones, all at my legs. They started to pry cobbles up from the street and throw them with more and more venom. They were children! What could I do? Then one took aim and hit me right in the temple, knocking me to the ground. Once I'd gotten my wits back, I jumped back up, ready to kill the four of them and eat them raw. But one was already on top of me with a whip and he got me right next to the eye. It whistled a little in the air and when it cut into my brow, I almost passed out from the pain. There was no one else on the street—killings tend to spook the neighborhood—just the four kids and me. I leapt forward as if I'd never forgotten the beast I once was and threw myself upon one of their necks, ripping out a piece of flesh, making a hole through which the rest of his life followed. I kicked the one carrying the whip right in the forehead, his pretty, well-bred forehead, and he fell down, stone dead. The others ran away, shouting that there was a travesti behind them, and I heard the rumbling on the cobbles and knew they were coming for me. When I got to the apartment, I found my son tending to a large gash in my husband's back. He had been pointed out at work as one of the disgraced. The women had told him to leave, and as they chased him out they threw a large computer at his back, opening up a wound that looked like a promising precursor to wings.

So we ran. We just ran.

We left behind our microwaves and hydromassage baths, our laser hair removal and plastic surgery, the comfortable sofas on which we'd made love, our warm showers when we got home, the closed windows that kept us warm in winter. On my desk I'd left the tickets to the play my husband and I were going to see the following weekend and a warm mug of tea we'd made to soothe our son's nerves. The photographs, the dresses, the underwear, exotic soap, mementos from our travels, and the bathroom screen with the image of Mount Fuji. My son cried over his toys, his sketchbooks, the drawings we'd stuck on the walls. Over his friends, who had thrown stones at his head in fear. His teachers, who had removed him from the assembly hall, forgetting the many times they had consoled him in his school life when he had been teased for being the son of a legitimate travesti, not a banned one as he was now. My husband was silent and wide-eyed. The bird that had brought warnings and changed colors fluttered over our heads. It was anxious for us to escape. We took the stairs having disguised ourselves as best we could so our neighbors wouldn't recognize us. When we got to the street, we were met by a different kind of silence, something lush and dense, like envy. Our car, which I'd bought in twenty-eight payments with my journalist's salary, was in a parking lot that we didn't dare enter because we didn't know how the attendant would react. We skulked along, sticking close to the walls in a city that was coughing up shootouts and the cries of travestis begging for mercy all around us. My son didn't want to keep going. He said he was staying, he wouldn't take another step, it was all my fault. We couldn't carry him. We had brought food, water, and warm clothing and it weighed as heavily as the recent dead. I begged him not to raise his voice, not to cry, someone might hear. My husband wasn't so patient and he smacked him. He smacked our son, whom we loved more than anything. My son cried out and my husband covered his mouth with an enormous hand more used to caresses. He looked the boy in the eyes and the message hit home. I don't know how long it took to get to the outskirts of the city, where women with scarves on their heads peeked out from behind their barred gates at the ghostly figures that roamed the streets. Travestis covered in blood, mutilated, some on their last legs and some soon to get there. Some very old, some not yet fifteen, some carrying their parents. There, we were able to rest for the first time.

One, recovering from the escape, said that they knew everything about us. Where we lived, what street, what floor and what apartment, where we worked, whether we had family or not, when we left the house and when we came home. Also that the goal was to deprive us of La Machi, who was the first they wanted to kill to disorient us.

"I tried to call the police when they came to burn my house down, but they just laughed and hung up," said a travesti, who was bleeding all over while one of the women from the outermost suburb of the city tried to stanch it with rags soaked in alcohol.

The local women came running to give us things they'd almost had to smuggle out of the house. Water, sandwiches, alcohol, antibiotics, and bandages. It wasn't yet dawn. The night would protect us once again. We were tending to the wounded, trying to understand what had happened, to decide where to go next, when an eleven-year-old girl appeared. When she saw us, she fainted with a groan. My husband picked her up and found that she had bruises all over her body. Her pants were covered in bloodstains. My son was stunned speechless. The women who had helped us were expecting new waves of fugitives who needed their help. They seemed organized but also afraid to be doing something illicit.

"We're not touching you," said one of them, holding up her palms to prove her innocence.

"No, we haven't laid a finger on you."

"We need to escape into the country and we need to do it now," my husband said imperiously.

We asked the woman to let the others know where we'd gone. We trusted them without knowing why. We kneeled in thanks and went on. I started to shepherd the others and, lame, mutilated, crushed and weak, we took the first steps of our exodus. We got past the beltway, jumped over fences, and headed deep into the countryside. Soon the sun was casting our long shadows over the grass. They no longer looked human. In the distance, we heard sirens, the shrill voices of the drones, gunshots, and blood-chilling screams. And then a cry much closer by, here, in our group, "Daughter!"

It was my mother. She had managed to escape. She ran into my arms like a girl reunited with her mother after losing her in a crowd.

We walked for hours, avoiding all signs of human life, skirting roads and wading through swamps. My mother coughed and kept the details of her escape to herself. Every time I asked her how she had gotten away, she just shook her head. She spoke with others who had joined our exodus, going from travesti to travesti, gathering facts, developing theories, and confirming suspicions, and then came back to me to report her findings. So I'd write them down. So that literature would remember through me. We went underground, over the roofs, hidden in the trunks of cars, in trash bags. We fled in whatever way was available to us, covered in rags, making ourselves nothing. We left through the sewers. We were hounded by those trying to kill us; their dogs had our scent, drooling over our flesh. We could barely walk with the little we had salvaged from our lives, the little we had managed to grab.

A group of assassins caught up with us on the edge of the bush, and we had to fight tooth and nail. Many died. We also saw the elderly bodies of our mothers die. Mine cried out and dropped dead, her back riddled with bullets. My son tried to break free of my husband to run to his grandmother but his father was too strong and dragged him into the thornbushes. I pleaded with them to stop, saying she was old, none of this was her fault, she wasn't anyone's mother, she was senile and running away out of dumb fear, but the men and women hunting us were deaf and blind.

I cried as we went on; I couldn't stop. We were headed for the sierras. The stone paths were silent. We climbed the mountain and the forest of ferns hurt us with its fauna. The bats drained us. My son couldn't sleep. Often, he didn't want to walk any farther. My husband picked him up. The girl he had carried since the city had died hours before. It was some time before we realized that she had stopped breathing. Like Lot's wife, I turned around many times to say goodbye to my home in Sodom. I expected to be turned to salt, to be frozen in place like a tree, but no, that wasn't to be my fate. It wasn't what they wanted. I don't know who was looking out for me on the other side. Maybe the legions of spirits we fed at home. When we felt that we had gone far enough, under a midday sun that threatened to burn us alive, we made improvised tents of dresses and blankets and rested until night came. We didn't light fires out of fear that the glow would give us away but we sat in a circle to reflect on what had happened.

Our cell phones started to go out one by one. Nobody slept a wink that night. The Evil Light cavorted around us like an ember dancing girl. Before dawn, we gathered our rags and went on.

Soon we came to Pampa de Achala and felt cold and unnerved. My husband, who was a keen rock climber around the city, said he didn't recognize the jungle in the distance.

"It wasn't there two months ago," he said, and the other men with us nodded. "But we need to keep going anyway."

"It's not a mirage," said a travesti voice from behind us. It was La Machi, who was riding on the back of an enormous dog, almost as big as a mule but much faster. A white dog with dark spots. We all kept quiet as she rode to the front of the caravan. She was carrying a bag of loaded shotguns and handed them out to those who knew how to use them.

"If you stop feeling sorry for yourselves for a moment, you'll realize that the land is telling you where to go."

Several of us collapsed, falling to our knees as though we were in the presence of an angel. Many of us had never seen her before. Many of us were expecting her when all the shit began, thinking she'd save us with her magic, the spells she'd learned and invented in her many years on the earth, but she was old and recovering her strength somewhere else in the country. She couldn't hold back all that evil on her own. But here she was, she had arrived and, seeing her sitting on her dog, with her chameleon birds flapping around her head, was like seeing a vision of God.

La Machi knew the land well. She had grown up at the top of the mountain, above the rocks, streams, and springs, beyond the pampas whose thick grass cut our bare legs. She warned us about snakes that left you writhing in endless agony. Scorpions that rotted you in seconds with their sting. We followed her. For the first time, I fell asleep still walking. My husband and son didn't realize that I was sleepwalking next to them. After many hours cutting our feet on the sharp stones of this new landscape, La Machi called a halt to our march and stroked the vegetation. She put her ear to the ground and heard the sound of roots bursting with youth and strength; she saw the wounds made by shoots breaching the surface. She started to murmur her familiar refrain, *Naré naré pue quitzé narambí.* The lullaby put us to sleep and when we awoke, thick walls of trees separated us from the world.

This was where we made our home. On the first day, our family's bodies rejected the change. The climate was different and dangers we had long forgotten now lurked among us once more. We didn't know how to cover ourselves, how to make a roof safely, where to point our windows. Then came the second day and our thoughts turned to food and drink. We went out to get to know the area. Soon came the third day and my husband was in the mood to make love, as I was to please him and, dirty as we were, we remembered what it was to thrust and withdraw and lick and bite, although we were disgusted by the stink from our mouths and armpits. On the fourth day it rained and we got soaked like newborn babes. We cried. We all cried. The men cried hiding their faces. On the fifth day, we dried all our things in the sun, including ourselves, naked in the jungle like armadillos. We dried our grief, carefully folded it up, helping each other to take it by the corners, and placed it underground. On the sixth day we looked alive again and some went out to hunt and cooked over fires that stretched far into the night. The tribe of outcasts was that large. Moving from fire to fire, the exiles asked each other whether they'd seen this or that, what things were and how they were named. Sometimes someone ran into someone else's arms and I took my son in my own, not out of love but loneliness. My anguish was such that I needed my son with me, between my breasts. I wanted his landless body next to mine.

La Machi rode out regularly on her enormous striped dog to look for the wounded and the lost, everyone who had touched us more than thrice, who were headed here, guided by the birds. She crossed through the wall of thornbushes that surrounded us and brought them to the camp, which soon swelled with refugees. During those first few weeks of new arrivals, she never rested. We wanted to go with her but she refused our company and headed out on her rescues alone with her soul, loading those unable to walk any farther onto the flanks of her dog. Here, we saw to our wounds, shared water, warmed each other up and cooled each other down, depending on the whims of the weather. We were already developing customs. We made an effort to tell the story every full moon. We gathered together for it, telling it from the beginning: what we saw, what we heard, what they did to our skins, the scars from the whips, and also those left by love. Little clans around the fire recounted everything we remembered and even began to make things up until we fell asleep. I listened out like an antenna dish; I wanted to hear and remember everything, everything said at these gatherings, because then I'd write it all down. Even if it was just scratched out in the dirt for the wind to blow away, I would write it down.

———

The jungle is everywhere. The undergrowth never seems to end, the thorns that scratch you as you run through them, away from an animal, or chasing one, or just trying to scare off the beasts so they won't eat the transparent bird I mentioned, one of the few left in the world, which has settled in my house. They say that the bird is related to Quetzalcóatl, who was in turn descended from the great Phoenix. The bird is still around because it lives underground, it digs its own burrow. This bird, a feathered chameleon that can change its size from as small as a sparrow to as large as an eagle, lives with me and its mood defines the atmosphere of my exile. When it is not assaulted by restlessness or sadness, its wingspan is similar to that of a man's embrace. Its tail must be three feet long, and its beak changes color to match. When there are hunters close by, it turns orange, like the evening sky, and you have to run like a lizard and pray to your ancestors, otherwise you're liable to end up on the end of a spear. When it sleeps it turns jet black, like a witch wrapped in her cloak. It moans like an old man. It came here as though it belonged solely to me. It left La Machi, earning me her resentment. She's upset, saying that I stole her offspring, but she's forgiven me because of what I've been through. She may not have accepted losing the bird, but I am its home.

In the beginning, we were the new arrivals, the strangers that stank of ass. The weather changed year after year and its cruelty arrived without a sound, like heartbreak. We stayed here and knew that the land was protecting us with thornbushes that formed a wall around our camp. The ones who stayed behind in the cities were afraid to come looking for us. Their satellites, watches, and cell phones didn't work out here, their technology refused to give us away, and they were afraid. They were right to be. When they sent out expeditions to track us down, they were never heard from again. The earth swallowed them whole.

Some of us started to lose our hair and we used the strands to make nests for our children. We covered our heads, ashamed of being bald. We were hairless and alone. We missed our makeup, our oils, the creams we rubbed over our bodies, the different blushes, the eye shadow. We grew ever more naked in the jungle; the harsh sun scorched us, and so did the cold. Our lips grew so dry we couldn't smile without bleeding, our skin burned, in one year we aged five hundred, our bodies were handfuls of dirt.

One day, a travesti with healthy curves came out naked but covered in mud with spirals drawn in her mud-caked skin. Etched onto her belly, shoulders, and back. Another followed her example, and then more and more and soon we all wore makeup again. The mud dried on our bodies in different ways; some were pale, others gray, others black. Some found brick dust from the ovens we'd used to build our temples, while others used their knowledge of the young landscape to make green and red inks for our new flesh. We shaded our brows and reddened our lips with blood from our gums. The hands that touched us said that they'd never felt anything so soft, we were like dust. We left parts of ourselves in everything we touched. Like a travesti curse.

Following on closely, almost at the pace at which we shed our trails, came the fox with whom I profaned my mourning period for my husband. He stalked me, constantly spying on me, his eyes fixed sharply on my bald head. According to the fox, he'd liked me the moment I arrived, only he was deeply wary because he mistrusted humans and wouldn't come any closer. But I didn't believe him, his fur had a deceitful stink.

What did it matter, after my husband had died— I'll write about it later on, I promise—I opened the curtains of my hut, the hut of a widow covered in mud, weeds, and straw, with which I cut gashes in my hands, gashes where I bled and rotted. The sheep came to lick the wounds. I had become a whore; I couldn't stand the urge to give him everything.

"What do you want from me? What do you want me to give you? My life, my house, my name? Tell me, because I don't know," I pleaded.

And now nothing was left on my lap but resentment. Hatred. I wanted him to look at his reflection in the river, all of it, to see every last inch, to have no escape from himself, from what he was, from top to bottom, from the most beautiful hair his mother gave him to the filthy paws with which he dirtied my home.

But anger is written drop by drop. This isn't the time to write my anger.

My back curved, my hair went gray. My breasts grew thinner and longer with bitterness. I became what I am now. I have surrendered to the tyranny of minerals and blind beasts. My feet sink roots with every step, it is hard for me to give up my love for the land, the roots draw up secrets from the mica, worms whisper my name. I keep taking one step after another, my breasts weigh heavily, my ass drags, my penis hangs dead underneath the skirt that protects me from mosquitos, wasps, and snakebites.

I miss the old sanity. I miss the cities like crazy. The city, which bustled with people, cars, and public transport. I miss the order of the cities at night, every criminal in their proper time and place, the whores gracing the street corners like an accessory to the moon, high heels echoing off closed storefronts and metal shutters. The sudden moans of a couple making love, maybe a few floors down, the laughter of my queer friends carried down the street on the east wind. Here, at night, the rattlesnakes give concerts and their repertory is maddeningly poor. Their voices seep inside you and make your life ugly. And the mosquitos... I hate the mosquitos and having to burn dung just to keep them away for a few hours. I loathe mosquito bites with my entire soul. In my first year here, I thought I would go crazy every night. I even cried in my sleep at my impotence in dealing with insects who seemed to want me the way I had once wanted my husband. Occasionally the hunters come. Men who can't accept our continued survival, even in exile. If you're caught by a hunter, it's better to swallow your tongue than stay alive for their entertainment. Many have died at the hands of a hunter. But none of the hunters has left our jungle alive.

I was grieving for my husband, who slipped as he was running to save our son and smashed his head open on a rock. The grief was like music, very fine parchment whose company replaced the life of my husband. I was a bearded widow. I was crouched down to pee by a molle tree when I heard twigs breaking under the heavy footsteps of a man carrying a rifle. I ran, piss running down my legs, with the hunter on my tail. I was going to die covered in piss. *He's going to eat me, he'll chew me up whole,* I thought as I slipped into a cave the hunter was too big to fit into. I sealed up the entrance with a stone. I was in there for three nights, my only nourishment tadpoles scooped from a pool. Occasionally, I gave myself a little light with a lighter that had almost run out of fuel. Three days later, the color-changing bird squawked at the entrance and I knew the coast was clear. I walked back with the burden of my humiliation, which was as heavy as my pain. I stank of shit and suffering. I walked back along the path down which I'd fled, jumping at every sound I heard.

When I found them in a clearing, in the shadow of a stone shaped like my face, I stood still. I didn't want to let them know I was there. A pig and a feline fully engaged in the act of love. I shan't deny to anyone that it made me horny, even with the stink of shit in my skirts, even with the smell of piss and bad breath from not rinsing out my mouth for three days. Even in my fear, I stood still as a statue, breathing so quietly that Death danced a Peruvian waltz, spying on the love between a cat and a pig. They reminded me of what it was like to fuck my husband. And also of shame, which I thought I'd long since shed. Over my impertinence. Wandering around, sinking roots wherever I liked, as though the jungle belonged to me. It happens. Sometimes I go out convinced that I'm no longer flesh and bone. I'm more like a mistake, a wayward spirit, alone, the silly bird crouched humbly on my shoulder, black and lazy like a pirate's parrot, like a military honor for having survived the next world. The bird that right now looks as if it's made of glass beads, a tasteless trinket.

Oblivion would have been preferable to the sullied love he gave me, which he left in my hands like a handkerchief. He brought it to my door when he heard I was a widow. If I had been the woman I am now, I wouldn't have given him a second glance. But I was alone and the death of my husband left a void full of electric shocks and burns. Why. I still wonder in the night, on the pile of grass on which I rest my body, why did I let him in. What was the point of lying to myself, telling myself that what I felt for him was love and that he loved me too. For those bright eyes that were good for nothing, not even seeing at night, nights that grew longer and longer. He acted as if nothing was happening, staring at his reflection in the river like a worthless Narcissus, adoring himself alone, envious of our travesti realm.

A smuggler very dear to us brought candy. He slips his way through the undergrowth without a scratch. He has long nails, which he bites off sometimes, but prefers them long. Sharp and tough, they're useful for defending yourself in the jungle. He can imitate the cry of a lapwing perfectly. When my bird hears him, the haughty creature turns blue and gold, as though it knew it were the most beautiful thing on earth, and I know that the candy smuggler has arrived. I gather together peaches, oranges, mistol beans, and the gold dust we steal from the river. I carry them in my skirt, with my hairy legs, the little hair I have left on my head, and my paws black with dirt. I go to him. He gives me a smile and a bow. His arm is so elegant and dapper, like a limpid flower, a stone in the river, that it appears to grow longer before my eyes. The others, just as earthy as me, come in long strides, their daughters dragging their hair behind them. It's a shame to see how the children ruin their hair.

"Hey, my lady, how do you chew?" asks the red man, the smuggler.

"Through sheer force of will," I answer.

I walk away slowly with the others; it's as though we're on a procession through a sacred forest. I suck on the candy as I watch the sweetness go to their heads.

The smugglers bring medicine, Coca-Cola, candy, books, candles, makeup, gossip, musical instruments, paints, pencils, paper, hot water bottles, mirrors, photographs from our abandoned apartments, whose owners are sometimes still here, alive and kicking. Smugglers bring luxuries and joy. They take away a kiss or two that will burn them for life.

The woman came to my door making a racket. She beat at my windows, a tangle of branches, thorns, and chrysalises, with her fists. She banged and called out in many voices for me to come to the door. I got up, gathered my breasts, and went to see the woman with her earth-caked face and cleavage. She was scared because her girl wouldn't stop vomiting. Her name was Lilith and I remembered her from the exodus, helping me get my son across one ravine after another. Here in the jungle, she met a professional athlete, I can't remember whether she was a boxer or a marathon runner. She had thick, muscular legs. They fell in love about two years after our arrival. Their wedding was a grand occasion. Shortly afterward, a younger travesti got sick and because we didn't have any medicine or magic (we invented the magic later), she died, leaving her small daughter—a girl she had picked up in turn on our flight into exile—orphaned and Lilith and her sporty wife adopted her. Just like that. Now that I write it down, I'm amazed by our simplicity.

Lilith's wife was warmhearted and a good talker. They went out to hunt and fish together and sold cleaning materials that they smuggled in. One afternoon, the woman caught a travesti stealing one of her hens and tried to chase her off but the travesti was armed with a machete, and although she only meant to brandish it as a threat, she ended up cutting the woman's throat. That's what happens when you run with sharp objects. It was a big tragedy. The whole jungle remembers Lilith's scream when she touched the pool of her wife's blood on the earth.

Poor Lilith, my widowed sister.

"She's puking!" she screamed at my door. "She's nauseous, she says she wants to jump out of her skin!"

She was talking about her daughter. She said she was sick. I don't know why she came to me instead of someone else, like a doctor, some of us were doctors. But no. She came to me maybe because I spoke to her daughter. I had taught her to read and write; she trusted me. I wondered what could be wrong with her. I got dressed, pulling strips of cloth over my naked body and tying them at the top and bottom. I got to the door of their house full of memories, mentally writing down all the words that had brought me to that moment.

"I haven't seen you in so long, and now look what I'm bothering you with," Lilith said. "But you gotta do what you gotta do."

Something's off, I thought, narrowing my eyes like a cut-rate detective looking for a nonexistent clue.

The girl, who looked green around the gills, was sitting under the awning, feeding the dogs pieces of bread with polenta and bones. Her gaze was sickly and her teeth were suddenly stained. She looked swollen, like a dog with parasites. I went to her and asked a couple of questions out of Lilith's earshot. The mother couldn't hear the answers either. When I was done talking to the girl, my suspicions were confirmed.

"There's nothing to be done, she's pregnant. At least twenty weeks."

The news didn't seem to come as a great surprise and Lilith immediately started pulling on her daughter's hair, shaking her as if she was trying to dry her out in the wind, and the girl screamed and bit at the air, trying to defend herself. They should build coliseums for fights like these.

"Let her go, you're going to hurt her!" I shouted.

"How did you do this to yourself? What happened?"

I was already on my way home but without turning around I told her that she knew perfectly well what had happened to her daughter. Milk had spurted into her body and taken hold somewhere in her intestines, a womb of shit harboring life. An ominous ovule had fooled a spermatozoid.

"Where will it come out? She'll die!" the grandmother-to-be cried.

"We'll see. She'll probably shit it out," I told her, grabbing a carob pod and sucking on it discreetly.

She started to throw stones at me.

"Resentful bitch!" she shouted. "I'm not coming to you anymore! I want nothing more from you! You're a bad influence, you brought us here and now we have no men and we live in fear."

"But it was the men we were afraid of, Lilith," I answered.

"Why did I follow you?" she screamed, tearing at the few hairs that still dangled impudently from her head.

"You didn't follow me, you followed La Machi."

"Don't you see, you stupid travesti? Don't you know?"

"Shhh, shhh, you crazy old man. Let us live in peace," her daughter interjected.

The girl had an ass of steel. She had discovered sex and she liked it, a lot. She waited for her lover at the edge of the barrier of vegetation. The jungle was forbidden to everyone other than smugglers and those who visited us bringing love. Lilith had no idea, but the whole jungle knew. The beasts of the forest mingled promiscuously, boar with cats, travestis with smugglers and the headless men who followed us into exile. Travestis with other travestis, travestis with the husbands of other travestis, the forbidden travesti with the forbidden fox.

Lilith's daughter was the lover of a headless man called Rosacruz, who came to our jungle via an underground tunnel. The girl wanted him; she went looking for him and lied to her mother. In the life before, other women also lost their heads for the decapitated men who had lived in our country for several generations. People said that it was like fucking honey, they were so sweet and sticky. She waited for him close to the wall and sometimes fell asleep. He sprouted from the soil like a mole, with his stub of a neck, clambered up, and would mount her for hours. Confused by her cries, which could just as easily have been out of pain as pleasure, we poured buckets of freezing spring water on them, we hit them with branches to see if we could distract them, but love was such a rare commodity, the desperation was such, that they didn't give in and we left them to rut like dogs. We kept the secret from Lilith. Like every mother, she knew nothing about her daughter's life. Her wife, the late athlete who died over a chicken, had told her, "You don't know anything about her."

What we never expected, what we never thought possible, was the pregnancy. How were we to know that our bodies, dry, clay vessels with pointless tits, were capable of creating life?

"This isn't an earthly event! It can't be! I'm going to poison the whore's food!" Lilith screamed.

Grandma Lilith, that was a sight to see! But the old woman could find no comfort. She screamed through the jungle, she stomped off into the carob forest, sending the guinea pigs scuttling away in fright. "She's going to die, the idiot's going to die! How's she going to get it out of her? And the father's nowhere to be seen, of course. Why did we have to end up here? We had to lose everything, to forget everything, start all over because of our desire and now this, even worse. Who will take care of me if my daughter dies? And with a headless man too, a shitty African, a penniless moron."

The egrets flew off, a blinding flash of white with long legs, like we'd once had on top of our acrylic stilts. Each of Lilith's cries lamenting her daughter's fate gave them an excuse to leave and never come back. We saw them go, white spots in a darkening sky filling up with stars. And as Lilith moaned and the village adopted new customs, the girl grew fatter and her stomach swelled. The travestis put their hands on her stomach, which wobbled in every direction.

What was gestating in there? The days passed and we found the need to invent some new mythology. To return to ancient idolatry. The pagan images, the ones Federico Moura sang about.

As we awaited the birth, we built a church in an abandoned brick oven. We had to remove the ash and coal and so got covered in soot, blackening our heads and bodies and sticking our eyelids shut. We went there to pray, or rather to sing songs from other lives we still carried around with us. We were heard: the rain came to our homeland and watered the deepest roots of the jungle trees. *Siquisiquisiqui,* the snake rattled, handing forbidden fruit out to the populi. Our mothers appeared in our memories, shrouded in old age and weakness. Our mind's eyes shattered with the memory of our mothers; we never thought we'd be able to revive the flame. At night, after my husband died and I had screamed and cried over him, a malevolent fox started to visit me. He had an enormous red cock. When I saw it for the first time, I cried on my knees, overwhelmed with excitement, "It's like Chinaski's cock! Red with purple veins!"

The fox was about five feet long and spoke kindly in a deep voice. Forbidden flesh, he said, bitch, horny ass, bitter old woman. The animal was five feet long and his muscles were firm, he was strong. If

I was hurt, his tongue healed my wounds, closed up my skin, soothed my burns. He made me forget my husband; he took my thoughts out to tour the jungle before returning them to my body. I pleasured myself with a jungle fox who knew my language, who knew how, where, and how long to plunge inside the swamp that I had become. The curve of my belly turned pink and smelled as good as his and so the music returned. Bitch against fox, we made music. I was shocked by the things I said to him, what my imagination was capable of. A long, thin tongue like a pink manta ray licked me inside my mouth, tooth by tooth, the whole arch of the gums, my sandy palate, the skin of my cheek, so similar to the inside of the ass into which he inserted half his beauty. I was revived. When he visited, the bird turned all orange, it glowed like twigs in a fire. I suspect it was jealous.

I didn't want to think about love.

We helped those who wanted to die. Those who came to seek our help would say, "I want bread." And we knew that they meant that they wanted to die, a condition from which travestis suffered, although we were never sure whether it wasn't a boon for us as well. One day, a travesti would decide when she wanted her life to end. They didn't want to die alone, so they came to us. We brought them to a stone house we'd discovered on the slopes of the mountain, who knows from how long ago. Men weren't allowed in. Just us and the women to whom we offered our help, doctors, psychologists, astrologers, chefs. We stayed with the suicidal woman until she'd asked for death five times. We tried not to get involved in the decision of those who came for help, we were just there, one of us walking with them, not letting them out of our sight.

Sometimes a whole troop of travestis would arrive and we would cook for them, making Pantagruelian feasts on long tables where we ate and chatted, everyone at once, talking over one another about the present, the past, and the future, envying the husbands and wives, showing each other the magical results of our surgeries, laughing and listening to the trees speak and the stones tremble. Those suffering from the urge to die were unfazed by the banquets; sometimes they laughed and I felt a crazy need to ask them that night how it was possible that women who had suffered so, who were about to take their own lives, could laugh that way, with cackles that scared off the ducks, who filled the sky with their quacking. Teenagers came, broken inside, they crunched when you hugged them, dry and weak, thrown out of their homes, raised in the wilderness. Old women came, convinced they were castoffs, the garbage of the world, ingrained with bitterness. Middle-aged women who had never been able to adapt came. None escaped the virus of suicide.

In a well-lit clearing, we gathered around the one who had decided that now was finally the time, that this was what she wanted.

"What drug do you want?" asked La Machi, who could get anything from the smugglers, even Lanvin and Guerlain perfumes.

The one about to die said, "I want acid."

We put the tab in her mouth and talked to her, asking about her childhood, and she would speak until she had found her state of grace. La Machi's eyes rolled into the back of her head, she dominated the scene. It could be hours and hours before the effect wore off and the suicidal woman went to sleep.

"For what they have done to us. For what we have suffered. For the bread they took from us. For the love denied to us. Let her go to travesti heaven."

She asked the observers to leave and, wielding a silver knife with a mother-of-pearl handle, whoosh. She was very precise, as though she'd been born to do it. She slit the woman's throat and it was done. We cremated them under a blanket of grass and prayed, *Naré naré pue quitzé narambí...*

I wrote in the earth with a stick, "What are all those travestis doing up a tree, like birds' nests made of sequins and synthetic leather? What are they doing there like fruit with cheap perfume, sparse hair, and thick makeup glowing in the moonlight? They look like panthers. They look like bats, hanging from a dream. What are they doing there, in a tree with dark bark that supports them like a hand holding a tangle of travestis in its palm? They're hiding from the police, that's what they're doing. They're terrified of the police, and so they climb trees like cats from the end of the world."

Every week, I go to pick up eggs at Sulisén's farm. Fresh eggs that she lays in the garden, grabbing hold of a post put there by her great love to hitch the horses to. She plastered the walls of her house with her bare hands, making the mud and smoothing it with her palms. Her house looked like one of us. Sulisén was one of the first to arrive and one of the first to cover herself entirely in mud. She had long, cracked breasts like mine, folds of skin cascading down from her shoulders. The skin got stretched by the implants and took it out on the nipples. Here, she settled down with one of the first men to come, one of those who'd touched us more than thrice. A hairy *chongo* with a back like an orangutan's who picked her up and made her caw when they made love.

"It was like he was throwing an orange up into the air and then boom! He'd slip in his dick without letting me touch the ground," Sulisén would say, giggling.

There's not much to say about their courtship, except that for a lot of us, the exile was better than before.

Sulisén's boyfriend was attacked by bees and there was no way to save him. He swelled up and was left fighting for every gasp of air until finally it wasn't reaching his lungs anymore. She was widowed and full of love that she needed to get rid of like old hair. The town fools wouldn't go near her, so we couldn't console her with fuckbuddies or jungle orgies and she faded and faded until she was skinny as a whisper.

She grieved over him for an entire autumn, sitting at the door to her hut. Sometimes we'd see her at the market or the mistol harvest and she'd never stop crying. Poor Sulisén. She aged a lot during that time. We watched her spend her entire life grieving for her dead boyfriend, on the porch, with fleas and ticks crawling over her feet. Every day she shrunk a little more; we could hear the crunch of her bones as her flesh contracted.

"Sulisén, what's wrong? Why are you crouched down like a hen laying an egg?" we'd ask as we passed by. Sulisén started her egg production in secret when she was still with the guy who died of the bee stings. She'd come over to visit and, every now and again, while we were drinking the coffee it was so hard to get smuggled in, she'd run outside, to the outhouse, and come back almost transparent.

"Girl! What did you have in your guts? You're all sweaty!"

"That's between me and my intestines," she'd say, carefully putting her satchel by her side, as if it contained something precious. One afternoon, when the summer had begun to feel more like prolonged torture than a season, she did it again. In the middle of our coffee, she got up, cutting me off just as I was relaying a juicy piece of gossip, and ran out back as if my coffee had made her shit herself. I followed her, making sure my feet didn't touch the ground, which can really give you away. I spied on her from behind a tree, not feeling the least amount of guilt. Her ass wasn't perched over the hole in the ground we used as a latrine. It was to the side, hovering close to the ground. Sweat glistened on her old skin. She took a deep breath and pushed until a chicken egg plopped to the ground and she carefully wrapped it in pages from a magazine she kept in her satchel. I stepped out because letting her know I knew didn't seem any worse than spying on her.

"Why didn't you tell me?"

Caught in the act, like one of those children whose mothers force them to pee in the street, she answered me in an arch voice, "What makes you think we need to know everything about each other? I have a right to my secret."

"But you're laying eggs, honey."

"I could be shitting gold and it would still be my secret to keep."

Her house soon filled with hens and roosters she didn't have enough hands to keep safe, not just from foxes, but from thieves too. Because even travestis can be criminals. We started working out a thousand ways to cook chicken, getting back the protein we'd lost in exile having never developed a taste for guinea pig. No meringue was ever superior to ones made with the whites of Sulisén's eggs. Never did a chicken re-semble us more than Sulisén's chickens. She named all the ones she could and she knew that it wasn't a crime to eat her offspring because she was a mother after all. Dada Breast, Cresty, Dirty Beak, Big Ass One and Big Ass Two, Mulatta, Chestnut Scratcher, Dodgy Guy, Raspberry Thorn, Red Feathered Fag-got, Coco Chanel, Pollito Ortega, Pollito Suárez, The One (That Crossed the Road), Pee Pee, and Pio Pio. The brood grew and there was enough for everyone.

Crouched down like someone with a whole life to mull over, she would wait to lay an egg, then another and another. Then she'd wash them. Sometimes she'd trade them for work, for someone to come sweep her garden or wash the meager rags in which she covered herself, to trade with the smugglers or fix her roof.

Sulisén greets me at the door of her hut, whipping up a meringue. Oh, it's wonderful to see her with so much energy, the hair on her forearm is black, a flea leaps among the hairs as if it wants to call attention to her dirtiness.

"What's up, Sulisén? May your days be cool."

"Nothing much, I'm just making the dessert for tonight."

Tonight, we're expecting the birth of Lilith's daughter's baby. Some of the older women are already with her, getting her through her first contractions. There are plenty of doctors in the settlement. Travesti doctors who do the best they can with the medicines that get smuggled in.

"Are you here for the usual?" she asks, knowing the answer. She hands me the clay bowl and the rusty whisk and tells me to keep whipping, it needs to thicken into snow, and goes into her hut. She's followed by a chick black as a crow. *Get out of here*, she says, pushing it away with her foot. She's so lovely with her chicken legs. She comes back with a dozen eggs. *They're clean*, she says, handing them over and taking back the bowl with the meringue whipped to perfection, the whites like snow. *No charge this time*, she says. To check they're thick enough, she turns the bowl upside down, and the whites stay put.

"Have you seen Lilith's daughter?"

"She's been pregnant for thirteen months," I reply. "Her breasts are full of milk. I don't think it'll be tonight, but it's a major event. Stay on your toes, Sulisén, things are getting better and better."

"La Machi says that it'll be tonight and I've always trusted her," she says. "I hope you enjoy the eggs now that you don't eat animals anymore."

It's true. I turned vegetarian after a fox ate my son.

We forge customs out here too. We built a nest here. Here, my son played in the gardens and kissed other boys, learning about love. We defended ourselves not just from the beasts but from the others too. From the travestis who accused me of setting a bad example by staying with my husband. Rolling around in the dust, pulling hair, we defended what others wanted to steal from us and we answered their insults in kind.

Just when I had gotten used to the music and the rituals, one night I was abandoned forever.

The boy was sleeping in the moonlight, covered by tulle from my skirt to protect him from mosquitos. It was my fault we let down our guard. I sought out my husband, who was just as old as I was, because that night, in the moonlight, he was the most beautiful man in the world, placed here on this earth, a lifeless patch of exile land, just for me. He was beautiful underneath the burden of the years that had flowed over him, sitting and looking out at the red night, smoking his pipe. It was my fault because I wanted to remember what it was like to have him inside of me, inch by inch, his curved penis, his almost yellowy flesh, the greenish veins underneath skin so transparent you could see his character. I rubbed myself with saliva, separated my buttocks and ate him whole as though I had teeth, little by little, to savor it, but eagerly, so he would be eager too, and he said he still wanted me very much and just then we heard our son cry out as he was taken by the fox.

My husband chased him all through the night, with me following after. We both shouted but no one came to our aid. For a moment, it was as though our old world had returned to us in the jungle. A lick of cruelty had leapt over the barrier of thorns. The vegetation felt as if it had sharpened its claws; it cut us and made us bleed. Scorpions and centipedes stood in our way, and the beasts growled in languages that are no longer spoken. He ran and leapt over streams until he got to the thornbushes that protected us from the hunters. The fox slipped in among them with my son clasped in his teeth and disappeared from sight. My husband was naked and scratched all over. I caught him up and like a coward who could do nothing for herself cried out, "Get him!"

He was jolted out of his shock and exhaustion. He pulled away at the thorns with no idea that there were daggers embedded in the trunks. He ran and, blinded by the thickets, slipped on some moss and split his head open on a rock.

Some time later, my fox lover, who relieves my pain over the loss of the child, took me to his cave. In one corner I saw my son's bloody clothes. I'm a bitch too, I recognized the smell of his blood.

To write this, I cleaned out my house. It took me days and days to get it clean, with a smooth, damp earth floor. I washed everything, even the nonexistent corners. I'm setting up altars for my son.

I skip out happily toward the ovens. The dandelions are in bloom, the lizard's tails are obscenely purple, and the grass is green. I pass other travestis dragging their hair behind them, leaving trails like snakes. They say that it scares off the animals and keeps them from attacking us. It's the same group that usually accompanies the suicides. The ovens look like our bellies in the sun, black and dry. The mother-to-be seems in good health. We've lost count of how many days she's been pregnant. Her belly is huge and thick, as though she's giving birth to a child of five or six rather than a baby. The headless father is with us. They say that they're a calm people, and it seems true, nothing affects his headless ways. The grandmother is a little more relaxed, resigned to her daughter's pregnancy. Lilith is lying next to the girl and soothing her with caresses.

"Be patient, go slowly. We're all here."

Sulisén arrives with her meringues and hands them out like Communion wafers. A doctor, one of our girlfriends, is checking her pulse, temperature, and contractions. La Machi is standing to one side, smoking her cigar as she murmurs her mantra:

"*Naré naré pue quitzé narambí. Naré naré pue quitzé narambí...*"

The headless man and inadvertent father, whose name is Rosacruz, is keeping discreetly back, according to custom, outside of the circle and the comings and goings of the travesti midwives. I bring him a little whiskey we've smuggled in and he thanks me with a bow.

"Everything's going to be all right," I tell him, but it's as though the words had slipped back inside, choking me. Rosacruz pats me on the back.

"San Blas, San Blas..."

La Machi continues her mantra.

This is like Chernobyl, the first time it has happened on earth. We are witnessing an event, a travesti giving birth. The day passes and suddenly shadows are lying down beside us. Lilith's daughter stands up, helped by her mother, and leaves the oven to stand under the tree. I feel too stupid to capture it in writing but I wanted you to see the pink light, the red of the edge of the wall, the stillness of the air, the girl heading for a molle tree and sitting underneath it. Rosacruz, her headless boyfriend, follows her, so polite he's striving not to crush a single blade of grass. We all crowd around to see.

The girl grabs hold of Rosacruz's shirt and groans and squeals as if someone has stepped on her toes. La Machi starts to sing and her eyes roll back into her head. A drunken hare passes by, crying out, "Night rooounnd, hoooowww saaaad yooouuu aaare, paaaassssing by my balcooony."

A contraction in the afternoon. I remember my son, my husband, the sobbing is more like vomit, I spit out the tears. I miss them, I miss my home in the city, I miss my bed and my bath. The time I spent with them, not so long ago, is still with me. I miss my parents, my friends, the ones I didn't find here. I miss the days at the beach, the sea, the bookstores where I could spend whole afternoons talking about writers. Lilith's daughter is in pain. But there's nothing we can do. We see the dance of instinct, the dust rising around the woman in labor. La Machi stops the doctor from going to help.

"Nobody move. She needs to do it herself."

"Someone, please help her," begs Lilith.

"She's with the father. They must know, they're not idiots."

Rosacruz turns to us and says, "It's born."

And he shows us the first pup, which is mewling the way puppies do. Then the girl gives birth to another pup and then another and another until her hands are full of six puppies covered in shit and a sticky goo like the inside of a leaf. Lilith wants to go over but the girl waves at her to stay where she is.

"This isn't the time," says La Machi. She stops her chanting and stretches out a hand. "Where's the whiskey, I'm thirsty. Leave them alone."

I stand back. Sulisén calls me inside, waving for me to drink wine with her. I go to drink with the others. Through the door we witness a landmark moment for our religion. The teenager licking her puppies and placing their muzzles at the six nipples that have appeared in her belly, full of milk, so they can feed.

CAMILA SOSA VILLADA was born in 1982 in La Falda (Córdoba, Argentina). She is a writer, actress, and singer, and previously earned a living as a sex worker, street vendor, and hourly maid. She holds degrees in communication and theater from the National University of Córdoba. Her play *Carnes tolendas, retrato escénico de un travesti* was selected for the 2010 National Theater Festival held in La Plata. Her first novel, *Bad Girls* (Other Press, 2022), won the Premio Sor Juana Inés de la Cruz and the Grand Prix de l'Héroïne Madame Figaro.

KIT MAUDE is a translator based in Buenos Aires. He has translated dozens of classic and contemporary Latin American writers such as Armonía Somers, Jorge Luis Borges, Lolita Copacabana, and Ariel Magnus for a wide array of publications, and writes reviews and criticism for several different outlets in Spanish and English including the *Times Literary Supplement*, *Revista Ñ*, and *Otra Parte*.